# the book of

# life

# KATHY LEE

© Kathy Lee 2009
First published 2009
ISBN 978 1 84427 369 0

Scripture Union
207-209 Queensway, Bletchley, Milton Keynes, MK2 2EB, England
Email: info@scriptureunion.org.uk
Website: www.scriptureunion.org.uk

Scripture Union Australia
Locked Bag 2, Central Coast Business Centre, NSW 2252, Australia
Website: www.scriptureunion.org.au

Scripture Union USA
PO Box 987, Valley Forge, PA 19482
Website: www.scriptureunion.org

The right of Kathy Lee to be identified as author of this work has been
asserted by her in accordance with the Copyright, Designs and Patents Act
1988.

British Library Cataloguing-in-Publication Data.
A catalogue record of this book is available from the British Library.

Printed and bound in India by Thomson Press India Ltd.

Cover design: GoBallistic
Internal design and page layout: Author and Publisher Services

✌ Scripture Union is an international Christian charity working with
churches in more than 130 countries, providing resources to bring the good
news about Jesus Christ to children, young people and families and to
encourage them to develop spiritually through the Bible and prayer.

As well as our network of volunteers, staff and associates who run holidays,
church-based events and school Christian groups, we produce a wide range
of publications and support those who use our resources through training
programmes.

# 1 The blind messenger

It was a blind man who brought the fateful message to the king. And I helped him. Afterwards, I thought it was the worst mistake of my life.

You can't go back and change the past. Later you look back and think, if only... If only he'd never made it as far as Embra... or if I'd walked right past him... or if the guards had turned him away at the castle gate...

But it was too late. What's done cannot be undone, as my granny always said. What's done cannot be undone – even when it's a knot around your own neck.

I saw the man standing on the quayside. I guessed he'd just come off the cargo boat that was moored there. He looked lost and helpless, which was not unusual when people arrived in Embra for the first time. The crowds, the noise, the smells of the city – it was all quite overwhelming, and it must be worse if you were blind.

No one was paying him any attention. No one stopped to help him... They had other things to do. I was in a hurry too. But I suddenly thought of our verse for the week. *Love your neighbour as you love yourself.*

"Are you all right?" I asked him.

He grabbed my arm as if it was an anchor to hold him in the flood of passing people.

"I must speak to King Andrew of Lothian," he said. "Can you take me to his castle?"

He had long, greying hair and a lean, weather-beaten face. A grubby bandage covered his eyes, like a sign to the world: *I am blind*. He looked like a beggar or a travelling musician – the bag over his shoulder was shaped like a guitar. Why would this man want to speak to King Andrew?

When I asked him, he wouldn't tell me. He said his news was for the king to hear – nobody else.

"What's your name, then, and where have you come from?" I said. "You sound like a southerner."

"And *you*," he said, avoiding my question, "sound like an islander from the far north-west."

He was right. But I'd been living in Embra for a year – long enough to learn a thing or two. For instance, listening to the sailors who were unloading the three-masted ship, I could tell they were from south of the border.

"You've come from Durham or Alnwick," I said. "What kind of music do they like there?"

The blind man laughed. "The same as everywhere. Songs of battle and bravery, loving and leaving. Now, are you going to take me to the castle? As far as the gate would be fine."

"I can maybe take you inside," I said. "I work for the king – I'm a boatman. But I don't know if you'll be allowed to speak to him."

The blind man thanked me. He held my arm as we made our way up the High Street towards the castle. Even though he couldn't see, I could tell that his other senses were sharp. He knew that I wasn't a full-grown man, although my voice had broken and my arms were strong from rowing.

"What's your name, son?" he asked me.

"Jamie Brown."

"And how old would you be?"

"Fourteen."

"And you're one of the royal boatmen? Can't the king get grown men to work for him?" he said, teasingly.

"I can handle a boat all right," I said, annoyed.

"You're lucky to land a job like that at your age."

"It wasn't luck," I said. "The king gave me the job as a sort of reward, I suppose."

"A reward for what?"

"For doing what you're doing. Bringing him a message." I didn't want to go into the whole story. It would take all day.

"Is that right? Well, maybe he'll have a place for a singer too."

The guards at the main gate knew me, but they wouldn't let the blind man in without asking his name and

5

his purpose. He gave his name as Sam Nightingale. A singer called Nightingale! It couldn't be his real name.

"And why are you here?" the guard asked.

"An old friend of King Andrew's is asking for help."

"Who might that be?"

"I'm not allowed to say the name to anyone except the king," the blind man said.

An old friend of King Andrew's – instantly I thought of Sir Kenneth. He had been the king's chief advisor for years, while secretly working against him. When his schemes were discovered, he had been put in prison. But he escaped and fled from the city. Surely he wasn't trying to get in touch with the king again?

After they'd searched the blind man for weapons, finding nothing, the guards let him pass. "Take him up to the inner courtyard, will you?" one of them asked me.

At the upper gateway, we were told that the king was busy. He was preparing to go on a journey – he couldn't possibly see anyone now.

"Take this to him. Then he might think again," Sam said. He took out a package of folded cloth and unwrapped it carefully. A small object fell to the ground.

One of the guards picked it up. It was a ring, a silver ring, small enough for a slim finger. It had a delicate, curving pattern around the outside.

"That looks like Norse work," the guard muttered.

"Take it to King Andrew," Sam said again. "It will prove to him that my message is important."

"Why should I? It's Norse. Maybe nobody's told you –
but we don't like Norsemen here in Embra."

"It wasn't a Norseman that gave me this," the blind
man said.

The soldier laughed. "Yeah. It was a Norse*woman*, I
bet."

"Not Valda?" another guard said, angrily. "She's got a
nerve to call herself a friend of King Andrew's."

Sam said nothing, but he gripped my arm tighter than
before.

"Captain!" the soldier shouted, and an officer came
out of the gatehouse. "Look what we've got here, sir. A
message for the king from that false-hearted
Norsewoman. Brought by a blind beggar from the
southlands. What action should I take, sir?"

"None at all, soldier. I don't think the king needs to be
troubled with this."

"But sir, I made a promise... " Sam protested.

"Get him out of here," the captain said to me coldly.
"That Valda woman has caused enough problems already.
It's best if the king never hears from her again."

# 2 The promise

"What am I supposed to do now?" the blind man muttered, as I guided him away from the inner gate. "I made a promise. I can't just walk off and forget it!"

"What was the promise?" I asked him.

He didn't answer. He stumbled over the slippery cobblestones, almost falling. I could tell that he was tired.

"Do you want to sit down and rest for a while?"

"All right."

I guided him to a stone bench close to the battlements. From here I could see half of Embra spread out below, with all its roofs, chimneys and towers. Sailing ships lay at anchor; small boats scurried between the islands like water-beetles.

It was strange to think that once, in the time of the Ancestors, the city had been even bigger. In fact, the whole country had been bigger. But that was before the world had got warmer, the ice had melted and the seas had risen up.

"Why was that guard so angry about the Norsemen?" Sam asked me. "In Durham, where I was born, there are plenty of Norse traders coming and going. And they never give any trouble... well, not until the pubs shut."

"It's not the traders that are the problem," I said. "Have you never heard of the Norse raiders? The other

Norsemen call them the Sea Serpents. They've been attacking the coasts of Scotland for years – ever since the seas rose up and drowned the best of their land."

"The Norsemen I've met weren't like that at all," said Sam.

"Yes, well... If you'd ever met the Norse raiders, you wouldn't be sitting here talking about it. Because you'd have been killed or sold as a slave."

"I sailed to the lands of the Norsemen, once," he said. "I spent a whole year there. Did you know that, in winter, it's dark nearly all day? And in summer the sun shines till almost midnight? Not that it makes any difference to me." He laughed.

He told me about the places he'd visited over the years. He would save up enough money to sail on a cargo ship and go wherever it took him. He knew the seaports of the distant south – Leeds and Reading and Milton Keynes – which were just names to me. And he'd gone even further afield. To Eire, land of a hundred green isles. To the pirate-infested shores of Russia and the desert lands of Spain.

"Then, in the end, I came home," he said. "Back to Durham. But Durham wasn't home any more. Most of the people I used to know are gone. My parents died long ago. My sister's married a rich man and doesn't want to know me. And Durham's changed too. It used to be a place where people knew how to enjoy life – not any more."

"So you went travelling again," I said.

"No. Not right away. I couldn't afford it. But then... "

His voice faded out into silence.

"Then what?" I asked.

"If I tell you what happened," he said, "can you help me to keep my promise? Can you take me to the king – or at least tell him my message?"

"Maybe," I said. I wasn't making any promises, myself. Not until I knew a bit more.

Sam told me that he'd been singing one day in the street outside Durham Castle. He hadn't heard much money being thrown in the bag at his feet, although he'd tried everything he knew. Old songs and new ones, an Irish lullaby, a Norse sea-song... but it was no use. People hurried past without even stopping to listen for free.

Then someone spoke to him. It was a man, asking if he knew any more Norse songs.

"A few."

"Would you come and sing them for a lady? You'd be well paid for your time."

He agreed at once. The stranger led him into the castle itself – he knew it by the sound of footsteps echoing under the arched gateway. And he began to feel nervous. The castle belonged to Sir John of Durham, a wealthy, powerful lord. If Sir John liked Sam's music, there might be a good reward. If not, Sir John might have him flung out in the street, along with his smashed-up guitar.

But he needn't have worried – he didn't have to sing for Sir John. He was taken up some stairs. A key turned and he entered a small room. There was carpet, soft underfoot, and the scent of flowers.

"My lady," said the man who had led him there – he sounded like an upper-class servant – "this singer brings you music from your homeland."

A woman, speaking with a Norse accent, asked him to sit down. He could guess who she was, for he'd heard people talking about her in the town. Her name was Valda, and they said she was very beautiful, with eyes the colour of bluebells and hair like white gold. Her father was a Norse trader, a friend of Sir John. It had been arranged that she should marry Sir John's eldest son, Sir Giles. But then Valda's father suddenly took ill and, three days before the wedding, he died.

The wedding was delayed for six months so that Valda could mourn for her father. It would now be held at the time of the great Autumn Fair. The whole of Durham was looking forward to the day.

But Valda – was she looking forward to it? Her voice, when she talked to Sam, was full of sadness. She sounded lonely and homesick, and the songs he sang her didn't seem to help.

"I would give anything to be at home again," she said in the Norse language.

"Then why don't you go back, my lady?" he asked her in the same tongue.

"I can't. I was promised in marriage to Sir Giles before I ever met him. But I don't want to marry him! He's a cruel man who cares about nobody except himself. I've seen the way he treats his servants. I am afraid he will treat me the same way."

"If you really don't want to marry him, you should tell him," Sam said. "Or just run away – why don't you?"

"You don't understand. They call me a guest here, but really I'm a prisoner.  The door is locked and there's always someone watching me. I can only speak freely to you because she doesn't understand our language."

Sam felt sorry for her. He couldn't see the beauty that everybody talked about. To him, she just sounded like a lonely, frightened girl.

"Is there nobody who can help you?" he asked her.

"There is one person," she said. "I know he would help me if he could. An old friend of mine – King Andrew of Lothian. But he lives far away in Embra."

"If I had the money for the fare, I could be in Embra within a week," Sam said. "And I would gladly take the king any message that you want to give him."

"Oh! Would you really do that? I can give you the money for the journey. Can I trust you? Promise me you won't let me down!"

"Yes. I promise."

He heard her count out some money. She slipped it into his hand, along with something else... a ring, it felt like.

"What are you doing, Lady Valda?" It was a woman's voice, speaking in English.

"I pay the singer," Valda told her. "I like to hear his music."

Then she said quickly, in her own language, "Go straight to King Andrew – don't talk to anyone else. Tell him that I still love him. Give him that ring and he'll know that I sent you. And ask him... beg him... to help me."

"I will," said Sam. "You have my promise."

# 3 The meeting

"So can you help me keep that promise?" Sam asked me.

"You make me want to help," I said, "but... "

"But what?"

I hesitated. "Well, I know why the soldiers didn't want you to speak to King Andrew. People say he's never been the same since the Norsewoman went away. He's restless. He can't settle down to anything. It's as if he can't forget Valda... she's always at the back of his mind."

"He would go to her, then, if he knew she needed him?"

"Like a shot. And he'd take an army with him. And then we might end up at war with the English, like we were 100 years ago - all for the sake of a woman."

"A woman who's already let him down once," said another voice, making the blind man jump.

It was my friend Rob. He'd come up the hill earlier, when Sam had just started his story. I had beckoned him over and Sam hadn't heard his footsteps - he had been too engrossed in telling the tale.

"Who's that?" Sam demanded.

"It's all right. I know him - his name is Rob. You can trust him like you trust me."

Sam looked doubtful.

"I've known him for years. We grew up together," I said. "Let me describe him to you... a face with more freckles than skin, red hair that doesn't go with the red uniform he's wearing... He's one of the king's messengers, by the way – he might be able to help you."

"What did you mean about Valda letting King Andrew down?" Sam asked Rob.

"He was in love with her. He thought she loved him, and he was about to ask her to marry him," said Rob. "Then she vanished. Her father's ship sailed away in the middle of the night, taking her with it."

"I don't know if she wanted to go," I said. "But she obeyed her father. He wanted her to marry the son of his old friend."

"If she really loved King Andrew, she shouldn't have cared what her father wanted!" Rob said. "She should have refused to go with him!"

"She is very young," said Sam. "Maybe she thought her father knew best. But now he's dead, and she's all alone in a strange place, among people she's afraid of. Please... let me tell King Andrew what's happened to her."

Rob and I looked at each other, undecided.

"At least take him Valda's ring," Sam pleaded. "Could you do that, without being stopped by the guards?"

"I'm a messenger... I can go anywhere in the castle." Rob thought for a moment. "I think the king should see the ring. It'll be up to him to decide if he wants to know more, or if he'd rather forget her."

Soon Rob came hurrying back, asking Sam to come to the royal chambers. King Andrew wanted to speak to him.

Sam gripped my arm. "Will you come with me?" he asked.

"Of course I will."

I should really have been on duty. The king had ordered his boat to be ready that afternoon so that he could inspect the progress of the new aqueduct. But somehow I guessed that his plans might have changed.

For the second time I heard the blind man tell his story. King Andrew listened closely. Although he'd ruled Lothian for several years, he was still only 21 – too young to hide his feelings behind the haughty face of a king. It was plain that Sam's story angered and upset him.

"Tell me again what she said – every word," he ordered.

Sam told him.

"And you say she's all alone... What about the other Norsemen, the crew of her father's ship? Can't she ask them for help?"

"I asked about that ship," said Sam. "I thought it might be the fastest way of getting here. I was told the Norse traders had gone to sea ages ago and hadn't come back. Maybe a storm took them."

King Andrew was silent for a while. Then he said, "What does Valda expect me to do? Send the fleet into

Durham harbour with guns blazing? I can't do that. I can't risk starting a war."

I heard a small sigh of relief from Rob, who was still in the room, awaiting orders.

"I don't know what she expects, your majesty," said Sam. "I only know that she asked for your help. She said you're an old friend of hers... "

The king laughed bitterly. "Yes, such an old friend that she left me without saying goodbye."

"And she still loves you."

"She said that?"

"Yes."

Another pause. Then, quite suddenly, the king came to a decision.

"Take messages to Sir George Duncan, General Macrae and Admiral Crawford," he said to Rob. "Ask them to meet me here this afternoon without fail. Don't say what it's about."

"Yes, sir."

"Go in person – don't send anyone else. The fewer people who know about this, the better."

In the afternoon I brought Sam back to meet with King Andrew and his chiefs of staff. Yet again he had to tell what had happened to him. And maybe it was a good thing he couldn't see the faces of the men who were listening. One looked furious, another was dismayed and the third seemed as if he didn't believe a word Sam said.

"Your majesty, I hope you're not going to pay any attention to this foolish tale," said Admiral Crawford.

"So you think the man is lying?" asked King Andrew. "I don't. Why would he want to make up a story like that?"

I didn't think he was lying either. I'd heard him tell his story three times, not word-for-word the same each time – that would have made me suspicious – but varying slightly as he remembered different details. I was sure he was describing something that had actually happened to him.

"All the same, there could still be trickery going on." It was Sir George who spoke. He was an ambassador, who travelled to foreign countries as King Andrew's representative. "I know Sir John of Durham. He would love to pick a quarrel with us. He barely has enough land to grow food for his people, and more and more of it is being destroyed in the search for iron and coal. If you give him an excuse to do it, he will make war against us."

"He wouldn't dare," growled the admiral. "We have guns and he doesn't."

The general said, "How can you be sure of that? Remember Sir Kenneth. We don't know where he went after he escaped from prison. He could have sold the secret of gunpowder a dozen times over. By now all our enemies could be manufacturing guns."

Sam said, "I've heard rumours that Sir John's soldiers have got new weapons. They can shoot three times as far as arrows. People say the iron foundries are working night and day to make more of them."

The admiral groaned.

"Well, that settles the matter. We can't risk using force," said Sir George. "Instead we should try diplomacy. Send me to Durham, your majesty, and let me talk with Sir John."

"What will you say to him?"

"I'll ask him to release the Norsewoman from her engagement to his son. I will offer him a good reward... say, a thousand Lothian cattle or two thousand sheep... or gold, if he prefers it."

King Andrew didn't like this idea much. "Valda's not an animal to be bought and sold," he said, angrily.

"I know that. But Sir John is a greedy man. Wealth and possessions are the things that he loves above all else."

"What if he refuses to let her go?"

"Then we'll have to think again," said Sir George. "But let me try the peaceful way first."

# 4 The book

In the next few days I often saw Sam around the High Street. He'd been well rewarded by the king for bringing Valda's message, but he was saving the money to pay his fare to somewhere else when he got tired of Embra. Meanwhile he sang in the street to earn his keep, and to pay a young beggar-boy who acted as his guide.

He was a good singer, I was surprised to find. If he'd chosen to be a musician in the house of some rich man, he could have had an easy life.

"Yes, but I would have been bored out of my mind," he said. "I like travelling around, visiting new places."

"Will you go back to Durham?" I asked him.

He frowned. "I don't think so. I don't like what Sir John has done to the place. People have more money these days, but they have to work hard for it. Their lives are nothing but work, work, work. They pay heavy taxes to Sir John. And there isn't the freedom that you have here."

"Freedom?" I said, surprised.

"Yes. You can do what you like and say what you like. It wouldn't be safe to do that in Durham."

I asked him what he meant.

"It's dangerous to say anything against Sir John and his men. If you do, something bad will happen to you. Like an accident at work – only everyone knows it isn't just an accident. Or maybe you just... disappear. It happened to a friend of mine. He went out one day and never came back."

"Do you think he was killed?"

"Nobody knows. He might have got sent to the mines." His face darkened at the thought. "The mines are terrible places, they say. People who get sent there don't come out alive."

"It sounds awful," I said.

"Yes. I like Embra much better." He started to pack up his guitar, for the shops were closing and the High Street was getting quieter.

The young beggar-boy picked up the money that had been thrown while Sam was singing. I saw him slip a couple of coins into his own pocket, and I drew in my breath ready to yell at him. Sam stopped me with a hand on my arm.

"Will you take me down to Annie's place?" he asked me. "Then I won't need my guide. He can get away home."

"Sure," I said.

Annie's place was well known to the beggars and homeless people of Embra. Anybody who was hungry could go there and get bread and soup, and a bit of floor to sleep on, if there was room.

"Sam, that young lad is stealing from you," I said, when the boy had run off.

"I thought so," he said, calmly. "But I don't grudge him a few pennies. I don't think he ever takes too much. And, if I hire somebody else instead, they might steal even more. Some people have to feel they're making a bit extra."

"Yes. Half of Embra's on the make, one way or another. They'd rob a blind man – they'd steal from their own granny. Embra's not really such a nice city, Sam."

"Well, nowhere's perfect."

Annie's place was at the bottom of a close – a narrow alley leading off the High Street. I knocked at an old wooden door in an archway, and Annie opened the door herself.

"Sam! Come in. And Jamie! Good to see you."

I had got to know Annie when she'd helped me after I was attacked by robbers. I still came back to see her quite often. She was one of the few people in Embra who would help a complete stranger... who would give the same warm welcome to anyone, from a beggar to a king.

The huge, high-roofed room was filled with the murmur of voices. There must have been 100 people there. Not all of them were homeless and hungry. Some, like me, had come to see Annie and to hear her read from the Book.

Reading, they say, was a common skill in the time of the Ancestors, before the seas rose up. But it had become quite rare, and books were even rarer. The secret of how to make them had been lost.

The words Annie read had been copied by hand from an ancient book, made in the time of the Ancestors. But the words themselves were far older than that. They'd been written in a time so long ago that it was past memory, in places I'd never heard of. And yet they often seemed to speak straight to my heart.

*If one of you wants to be great, he must be the servant of the rest... like the Son of Man, who did not come to be served, but to serve and to give his life to redeem many people.*

That was a hard saying, I thought to myself. But Annie had chosen it as our verse for the week. I would have to look out for ways to obey it. As Annie said, it was a waste of time hearing God's word if you didn't do what he said.

Sam listened closely and, when Annie had finished reading, he began asking questions. Who had said those words? What did they mean?

"It was a man called Jesus," I said. "Well, he wasn't just a man. He was the Son of God. And he could do miracles – he could make blind people see and lame people walk."

"What happened to him?"

"His enemies killed him. But God brought him back to life again."

"If he was here now," Sam said, "I would ask him to make me see again."

"You can still ask," I said. "He has promised to hear our prayers. A few weeks ago Annie prayed for a woman who couldn't walk, and she got better. Do you want her to pray for you too?"

I felt nervous as I said it. Sometimes, I knew, people did get healed after they were prayed for... sometimes they didn't... and sometimes it just took time.

"I don't suppose it will do any good," Sam muttered. "May as well try it though."

But no miracle happened. After people gathered around to pray, his eyes were just the same as before, and he gave a disappointed sigh.

Annie said, "I'd like to take you to an eye doctor that I know. He might be able to help you."

"All right," said Sam.

It was getting late. I said goodnight and hurried back to the castle. Soon the gates would be closing for the night and I didn't want to get shut outside.

I had a small room above the water gate of the castle – the fortified entrance where boats could be launched at high tide. I had hardly got there when I heard footsteps running up the stairs. It was Rob, looking excited.

He had to take a minute to get his breath back before he could tell me his news.

"The king's sending 100 soldiers on a secret mission to Durham! They'll go in disguise, riding with the cattle going south along the drove-roads. It's meant to look as if they're just guarding the cattle from the border reivers. But, when they get there, they'll try and rescue the Norsewoman!"

"Here, slow down. I don't understand what you're talking about."

"And I want to go too! I'm going to volunteer! Are you with me, Jamie?"

# 5 The drove-road

Rob began to explain. "Every summer thousands of cattle are taken south to be sold in Durham and Harrogate. To get there, they have to cross the wild hills where the reivers live."

I had heard of the reivers. They lived in the border country to the south. They hated the English lords, but they didn't obey the king of Lothian either.

"In the last few years," Rob said, "the reivers have attacked the herds, trying to steal cattle. The cattle-drovers asked the king for help, and he's agreed to send an armed guard this year. And then the soldiers will get into Durham by the back door – by land."

"Oh, right. Sir John would expect to be attacked from the sea."

"Yes. He's got ranks of cannon lined up on the hills outside the city, ready to blast enemy ships coming up the river. Sir George Duncan saw them."

"How do you know all this?" I asked him. (Stupid question. The royal messengers always knew much more than they were meant to.)

Rob said, "I heard Sir George making his report over the radio. He tried to get Valda released from her engagement, but it was no use. Sir John's determined that she'll marry his son."

"Why? If she doesn't want to marry him, it's not going to be a good marriage," I said.

"Kings and lords don't marry for love," said Rob. "They marry people who'll be useful to them. Sir John might want to make an alliance with the Norse traders. He could make sure they didn't trade in, say, sulphur, with anybody except himself. Sulphur comes from Iceland, one of the Norse lands, and you need it for making gunpowder."

I understood that part all right. If the king's scientists could not make gunpowder, all our guns would be useless lumps of scrap metal.

What I didn't understand was how a force of just 100 men could be expected to reach Valda. After all, she was inside a castle.

Rob laughed. "You could probably get into any castle with fewer men than that, if you came in peacetime and made a surprise attack. I mean, think of how Embra castle is guarded – half a dozen men at each gatehouse and that's all. We rely on the fact that our enemies can't just arrive here out of the blue. Our ships would stop them."

"All right, so they might be able to get in there and find Valda. They might even get her out of the city. But then what? Sir John and his men would be after them straight away."

"It's all been worked out. Our fleet will be waiting offshore, well out of range of the guns at Durham. If the soldiers can reach the coast, they'll signal and our ships will come in and take them away."

His eyes were shining.

"It'll be amazing, Jamie! People will tell the story for 100 years. They'll write songs about it. We'll be heroes!"

That was the difference between Rob and me. He wanted to be a hero – I didn't. I'd already seen that heroes mostly got killed before the end of the battle.

He said, "Oh come on, Jamie. I'm definitely going to volunteer for this, but it will be far better if you come too. You're not scared, are you?"

"If you had any sense, you'd be scared too. And what about going back home?" I had been saving up for months to buy a boat that would take us home to our island. I hadn't seen my family for over a year – they probably thought I was dead.

"There'll be time for that later. Just think of the tales we'll be able to tell them!"

Two days later, we were standing in line in front of the army headquarters. Rob, being Rob, had somehow persuaded me to go along with him and volunteer. I only went because I was pretty sure we would be turned down. We were too young, for a start. And we had no army training, although Rob was a good swordsman and I was quite handy with a bow.

"What are you doing here, sonny?" the sergeant asked Rob.

"Volunteering for the secret mission."

He laughed out loud. "It's soldiers we need... not half-grown lads that would fall over backwards if they fired a pistol. Get out of here!"

"Don't you think you might need messengers?" Rob said to him. "That's my job. And I can ride too. I bet half these soldiers of yours are city men who don't know one end of a horse from the other."

The sergeant was listening now, not laughing. He actually looked as if he was taking Rob seriously.

"And we know how to handle cattle," Rob went on.

"Who said anything about cattle?" The sergeant gave him a suspicious glance. Rob suddenly remembered that this was a secret mission and he shouldn't know anything about it.

The sergeant went away and talked to a senior officer. Then he came back. "We'll take you on as messengers," he said. "Collect your kit from the quartermaster – over there. And look lively! You're in the army now!"

So this was how we came to be riding southwards across the hills, part of a long column of men and cattle. There were more cattle than I ever knew existed – an endless stream of dark heads and tossing horns. We were driving them along a grassy road, so broad that it was more like an endless field, with stone walls on either side.

Riding at the centre of the column, you couldn't see where it began or ended. The drove road took it up winding valleys, over hills and even across rivers. The soldiers were spread out along the length of it. They were dressed like cattle-drovers, in old, homespun tweed clothes and thick woollen cloaks. They rode on shaggy hill ponies, not cavalry horses.

The real drovers and their dogs kept the cattle moving all day. They didn't go too fast, for that would make the cattle lose weight and fetch less money. They said it would take us a couple of weeks to reach Durham.

Each day's journey ended at a stand, a huge field where the cattle could feed and rest. The drovers wrapped themselves in their cloaks and slept in the open. The soldiers took turns sleeping and keeping guard, for we were coming into the border lands – reiver country.

So far there had been no signs of trouble. But then one day, riding at the rear of the herd, I looked back and saw a group of riders in the distance. I counted 10 of them, with a couple of packhorses as well. They seemed to be following us along the drove road.

The soldiers sent me to tell our leader, Lieutenant Fairfax. He took a group of men to guard the rear of the column. The riders were catching up with us, not even trying to stay hidden.

"They're soldiers," the Lieutenant said. I didn't know how he could tell, for the riders weren't in uniform. "Maybe they're bringing new orders from the king."

The foremost rider was a young man, dressed like a drover, with several days' growth of beard. I thought he looked familiar somehow. But it wasn't until he spoke that I recognised him.

He said, "Good afternoon, Lieutenant Fairfax. Could you use a few more men?"

It was the king himself!

"Your majesty!" The lieutenant sounded as surprised as I was. "Er... is this wise? We're on a mission of some danger."

"Oh, not again." The king sounded angry. "All my advisers keep telling me I must stay in Embra and keep out of danger. I'm not a child any more! How will I learn to lead armies, as my father did, if I am never to leave the city?"

I thought he had a point. But maybe that wasn't his real reason for joining us. Maybe he wanted to rescue Valda himself, riding in like some hero from the old tales. *Don't believe all the tales you hear*, I wanted to tell him. *In real life, not everyone lives happily ever after.*

The lieutenant said, "Who is ruling Lothian in your absence, sir?"

"My chiefs of staff. And we can keep in touch by radio. I've brought a new version of the radio that my scientists have been working on. It's amazingly light and portable – a packhorse can carry it."

It was quite plain that Lieutenant Fairfax was still worried. He didn't want to have the responsibility of guarding the king on this mission. But what could he do?

"Don't look so anxious, Fairfax. It's all going to be fine," King Andrew said.

He couldn't have been more wrong.

# 6 Night attack

When we halted for the night, the radio operator unpacked his kit. He fixed an aerial wire to a tree and turned the handle that powered up the radio. He soon had a crowd of soldiers around him, interested to see this new invention – which was really an old invention from the time of the Ancestors. The king's scientists had recreated it using books from the Old Times.

The cattle-drovers kept well away. They were probably afraid, like my own family would have been. In the hills and islands, anything from the Old Times was thought to be unlucky.

An old drover was sitting beside us as we ate our supper. Rob asked him if he'd done the trip south before.

"Aye. Every year since I was the same height as you are."

"And have you seen the reivers?"

"Seen them? I've more than seen them. I've fought with them." He showed us a long sword-cut on his arm. "Every year they seem to get worse. But maybe the soldiers and their guns will teach them a lesson."

It was beginning to rain. I wrapped myself up in my cloak and lay down, trying to find some shelter beside a wall. I wondered what the king would think of sleeping rough like this. It was a long way from the comforts of Embra – soft mattresses and velvet-curtained beds.

And, what if there was fighting, and King Andrew got killed? He had no son to reign after him. There would be several people in Lothian who might want to take the throne – powerful men prepared to fight for more power. It might end in civil war, with Lothian destroying itself.

"Rob," I whispered, "do you think the king was wise to come on this mission?"

"Maybe not," said Rob. "But, if I was him, I'd have done exactly the same."

I sighed to myself, and tried to get some sleep.


It was the gunfire that woke me, echoing between the hills.

I leapt up, tripped over my cloak and got up again. The noise was coming from the far side of the stand. Men were shouting. Hundreds of hooves trampled the ground as terrified cattle milled about, mooing loudly.

In the darkness and confusion, it was hard to know what was going on. More shots rang out. I bumped into Rob, who was carrying his knife at the ready. I was lucky he didn't stab me.

"They must be fighting off the reivers! Come on!" he cried.

He swung himself over the wall, and I followed him. At least we would be away from the cattle, with their sharp hooves and even sharper horns.

We went around the outside of the wall. What would we do if we met the reivers? Neither of us had a gun, or even a sword. Our knives wouldn't be much use against a gang of desperate robbers.

The firing seemed to have stopped. Then suddenly a shot rang out from inside the wall, just a few feet away. Rob dropped to the ground.

"Don't shoot!" I shouted. "Rob! Are you hurt?"

"No, I'm all right."

"Get out of the way, you young idiots," the lieutenant shouted.

It had been a close thing. Rob had almost got shot by our own soldiers. That would have been our only casualty, apart from the damage the cattle had caused, goring each other in their panic.

One of the reivers lay dead outside the wall. Others might have been wounded, but had got away. When daylight came, the soldiers examined the tracks they had left. There had been at least 30 of them, all on horseback.

The armed guard seemed to have taken them by surprise. "But they'll be back," the old drover muttered. "Or another lot will."

"Another lot?"

"Aye. There's half a dozen different reiver clans in these parts, all as bad as each other."

It was still raining as we set off again, and it rained for the next three days. The cattle didn't seem to mind. Like the drovers, they were used to being out in the rain. They plodded steadily along the track, which was now a brown swamp of churned-up mud.

I felt cold and miserable. There was no way of getting dry, even at night. Shivering inside my soaking wet clothes, I wondered if I would ever feel warm again.

It was even worse when we had to cross fords. With all the rain, the rivers were running high. The smaller cattle sometimes lost their footing and had to swim across. Cows are not afraid of water, but you couldn't say the same for the soldiers. As they walked their horses across, some of the Embra men looked very nervous.

"I don't know what they're so scared of," I said to Rob.

"Most Embra people never learn to swim," he said. "It's not their fault. The sea around the city is filthy. Would you go swimming in the sea if you lived in Embra?"

I thought of the beautiful, empty shore where Rob and I had learned to swim almost as soon as we could walk. Once again I was filled with longing for my home, for a warm fire and a roof to keep the rain out. Instead of going back there, I was travelling further away.

"I wish I'd never listened to you, Rob," I muttered. "I'm sorry I came on this journey."

"Well, I'm not," said Rob, annoyingly cheerful. "Come on, don't let a bit of rain get you down, Jamie. And there's one good thing about the weather – we haven't seen any more of the reivers."

"We haven't *seen* them... that doesn't prove anything. They could be following us at a distance, waiting for their chance."

I turned to look back along the track. The wind blew gusts of rain into my face. There was nothing to see except empty grey hills, black clouds, and rain.

"See? Nothing there," said Rob. "And in a day or two we'll be safely out of the border country."

I prayed that he was right.

Over a hill, into a new valley... the track went on and on. We were coming to another ford. This was the widest river we'd met. The water was swift-running and deep – much deeper than usual, the drovers said.

The king, the lieutenant and the chief drover discussed what to do.

The drover said the cattle should get across all right, although some might be swept down river and have to be rounded up.

"It's the supplies I'm worried about," said Lieutenant Fairfax. "We'll have to unload the packhorses and carry things across. Gunpowder has to be kept dry or it's useless."

"The same goes for the radio," said King Andrew.

"We could wait and see if the water level goes down in a day or two," Lieutenant Fairfax said.

The chief drover said, "That'll never happen if the rain keeps on. It's going to get worse, not better. And, if we wait here, what are the animals to eat? We have to keep them moving."

That settled it. We got ready to make the crossing. I took the orders down the length of the column and then rode back to the riverbank.

A rope had been tied across the water and made fast at both ends. It gave the men something to grip onto as they carried bags of supplies on their shoulders. The water was around waist-deep, racing along as fast as a horse could run. One slip of the foot and it would easily carry you away.

Meanwhile the cattle had started to cross the river. They climbed out on the far side, with flanks heaving and water streaming off their bodies. Slowly their numbers grew on the opposite bank. Slowly the herd on our side dwindled.

The king watched anxiously as the radio operator went into the water, carefully balancing the awkward-shaped package that held the radio. The man looked terrified.

He was halfway across when there was a sudden yell from the back of the column. "The reivers! They're attacking at the rear!"

Startled, the radio man looked round. He must have let go of the rope. Next thing I knew, he'd fallen sideways into the water, and the radio had gone with him.

"No!" King Andrew shouted. He leaped into the water, trying to catch the man or the radio, I don't know which.

But the swirling water was too strong for him. The man was carried away beyond his reach.

And now the king was in trouble too. Below the ford, the water suddenly got deeper. He was out of his depth. He cried out as the water dragged him down.

"He can't swim!" Rob yelled to me. "He'll drown!"

# 7 Caught in a net

We both dived in at the same instant. There wasn't time to feel scared.

But, when I felt the strength of the current, I was scared all right. It swept me along like a broken twig, far faster than I could swim. All I could do was try to stay on the surface.

I couldn't see King Andrew at first. I thought he must be already underwater. Then I saw him a few yards down river from us and I swam frantically, trying to get closer.

We reached him just in time. It was a good thing there were two of us, for he grabbed me with the strength of desperation and almost dragged me under. But Rob took hold of one of his arms, and between us we managed to support him in the swirling waters.

I tried to shout for help. But, when I looked back, we were already a long way from the ford, and getting further every moment. Had nobody seen us go in?

A few times my feet struck rocks, but we were moving too fast to be able to stand up. And now the water was getting rougher. I could hear the roar of rapids ahead.

"Quick, aim for the bank!" Rob gasped.

We kicked out as hard as we could. But the river was far stronger than we were. We couldn't make much headway, especially with the king clutching our arms.

The radio operator had managed to reach the bank. He was struggling out of the water as we swept past him, out of reach. His horrified face was the last thing I saw before the rapids took us.

*Oh God, help us!*

The dark river turned white with foam. It raced over the rocks in a furious torrent, carrying us with it. We were bashed and beaten against stones, dragged underwater and thrown up again.

It was a desperate struggle to keep air in our lungs, to stay afloat, and to hold onto King Andrew. The river was trying to rip us apart – but somehow we managed to stay together.

Between the rapids were calmer stretches, although never long enough to let us get our breath. Then came another plunge into the white water... another battering, bruising fight to stay alive.

At last the river grew quieter, running swift and smooth through a wooded valley. We made a new effort to swim ashore. But Rob and I had no strength left, and the king was like a dead weight in our arms, barely conscious.

I heard a sudden shout. I felt something catch me and hold me like a fish in a net. And then there were men around us, wading into the water and helping us onto the land.

"Biggest salmon we've ever caught!" somebody said.

The men, who had been fishing with a net stretched across the river, could see we were exhausted. "We'll get them home and let them dry out," said their leader, a black-bearded giant of a man. "Then we'll decide what to do with them."

Did these men belong to the reivers? I didn't know and I didn't care. They'd saved us from drowning. That was all that mattered.

Three of the men put us on their horses. They led us through the woods and up a side valley for a mile or two. Ahead of us I saw a strange building, part farm and part castle. We were taken into a stone-built tower, and made to sit by a fire. Two women brought us dry clothes and bowls of hot porridge.

I began to feel better. I was warm for the first time in days. And King Andrew was looking more alive.

"Thank you," he said to us. "I would be dead by now if it wasn't for you."

"We would all be dead if it wasn't for these people," said Rob.

"That's right," said the big man. "So maybe you owe us something. Maybe your friends would be prepared to reward us for saving you? That is if they want to see you again."

This was when it dawned on me that we hadn't only been rescued. We had also been kidnapped.

I looked at the king, expecting him to tell them who he was. But he frowned at me.

"We're just cattle-drovers," he said. "Our friends might pay you a few cattle. They don't have any money until they get the cash from selling the animals."

"Funny," the chief said to him. "You don't seem much like a drover to me. You're not sunburnt enough and you don't smell of cattle-dung. You look more like a soldier."

There was an angry growl from the men around us.

"News travels fast in the borders," said the chief. "We heard that the king of Lothian has sent in soldiers with guns. Now is that fair? Using guns against men armed with swords and spears?"

"Fair? Is it fair to steal cattle from the rightful owners?" Rob asked.

"Yes, if they won't pay us for travelling over our land and eating the grass that our herds could eat!" said one of the other men.

King Andrew said, "If you take us back to our friends, I'll make sure you are well paid in cattle."

"Yes, and then you'll make sure we get shot as we're riding away. I don't trust soldiers," the chief said, scowling.

"We could sell the three of them at the hiring fair," a woman said. "They'd fetch a good price."

Rob and I looked at each other in dismay. Sold as slaves! Now, surely, we should reveal who King Andrew really was? But he silenced us with a look.

The reivers went on arguing. We were taken downstairs to the cellar of the tower and locked in for the night.

"Why wouldn't you tell them who you are?" Rob demanded, as soon as we were alone.

"Because they would demand a huge ransom if they knew. And it might take a long time, maybe years, to arrange our freedom. Better to take our chances and hope we can escape. Maybe we won't be so carefully guarded if they don't know who I am."

In the darkness I was finding my way around the cellar. But there wasn't even a window. The only door was firmly locked.

"This is all my fault," King Andrew said, sounding depressed. "I'm sorry the two of you got involved. But I'll always be grateful to you for saving my life."

"You never know," Rob said brightly, and I just knew he was going to say something annoying. "Something good might come out of this. If we get sold to somebody from Durham, it might be another way of getting in there without being seen."

The king groaned. "That wasn't how I planned to arrive in Durham."

As we lay on the filthy straw that was the only bedding, I thought about what Rob had said. I had prayed for God's help in the river, and this was how the prayer had been answered. Could God really bring something good out of it?

"Trust him," Annie always said. "Trust him in the dark times and the good times. God loves you like a father loves his children. Even if it feels as if he's far away, he is always there."

*I will try*, I told him silently. *I will try to trust you, whatever happens.*

There were rats scurrying in the corners and fleas in the straw. But I was so tired that night that nothing could keep me awake.

# 8 Deep down

Two days later, we were at the hiring fair in a market town further down the valley. The reivers had made their decision – to sell us.

The market place was crowded. Men looking for work stood in line, carrying the tools of their trade. Cows and sheep were on sale in the centre. And in the corner of the square, people were on sale too.

There were about 40 of us, including several small children. Our hands were tied and our owners stood guard over us. So far there had been absolutely no chance of escape.

I was sitting next to a boy of about 8 and his sister, even younger. The boy said they were from an island far to the west. Their village had been raided by Norsemen; their parents were killed in the fighting. The Norsemen had captured the children and sold them to a slave dealer, who had brought them here to sell again.

"The man said we were the right size to work in a mill. What's a mill?" he asked me.

The only mills I'd ever come across were windmills that ground wheat to make flour. I couldn't imagine why children would be needed to work there.

The little girl began to whimper. "I want to go home," she said. "When are we going home?"

"We're not going back, Lizzie. Shush now."

"I wish Mammy was here," she said, and tears came into her eyes.

"Don't you cry, Lizzie. Don't you cry," the boy said. "Mammy's in a better place than this – the place where there's no more death or sorrow or crying or pain. And we'll be there ourselves, soon enough."

His words reminded me of something Annie had read from her book. No more sorrow or crying or pain...

"Do you mean heaven?" I asked him.

He nodded. "If you believe in God, you go to heaven when you die," he said. "Your name's written in the Book of Life and you'll live forever. So don't be scared of dying. That's what Mammy always said."

I wanted to talk to him some more, but there wasn't time. His owner kicked him.

"Come on! Stand up and look alive! We've got customers. And you, girl, stop snivelling – or I'll give you something to really snivel about."

A smartly-dressed man had arrived. He looked at the slaves on sale and didn't seem impressed. "Are these all the children you've got?" he asked.

The reiver chief pushed us forward. "Take a look at these young lads. They're good and strong."

"Too big," the customer said. "Far too big to crawl under the machines. They'd be more use in the mines – show them to my friend over there." He turned back to the slave dealer. "I'll give you 20 pounds each for those children."

"Fifty. I can't take less than 50," the slave-dealer whined.

"Twenty-five, then. But I hope they're better than the last lot you sold me. They were rubbish! If this lot are as bad, I'll report you to Sir John!"

The slave-dealer said hastily, "Don't do that, sir. I guarantee these are top quality. And look, I'll do you a special deal... "

At last they agreed a price between the two of them. The group of children was led away, and I watched them go. The young boy who was so brave... what would happen to him? He believed in God, and yet terrible things had already happened to him, and even worse things could be on the way.

Another customer started looking us over. I had a dreadful thought – we might be split up. All three of us might be bought by different people.

But this man bought all the men and boys who were on sale.

"We need more workers. The mine's expanding. We can't get coal out fast enough to meet the demand," he told the slave-dealer. "Get us as many slaves as you can – good strong ones, mind – and you can name your price."

We were marched away in a line, guarded by armed men on horseback. It reminded me of the cattle herd, but this time we were the animals being driven onwards to meet our fate.

On the second day of our journey, the landscape changed. Instead of green hillsides, there were heaps of grey gravel and earth. Instead of valleys, I saw huge holes that seemed to have been dug out of the ground. Black pools lay at the bottom of them.

The wind that blew in our faces brought clouds of dust with it. Soon it was hard to see the light of the sun. Everything was grey, dusty and dismal-looking.

We came to a massive iron gate, guarded by armed men. On either side were fences made of wire, stretching away into the distance. Beyond the gate lay a vast hole, as wide as a city, as deep as a deep well. The air was full of dust and grit, making me cough.

A track led us down into the pit. There were dozens of men at work with pickaxes and sledgehammers, barrows and sacks. Here and there stood guards carrying whips.

This was the mine. This was the place that Sam had talked about with dread. "People who get sent there don't come out alive... "

Before being put to work, we were fitted with iron collars that locked around our necks. Then the guards lined us up to be inspected by the manager of the mine. He was a sharp-faced, mean-looking man.

"Welcome to your new employment," he said. "There's nothing to fear here as long as you're prepared to work. You'll be treated well and fed well. But, be warned – we don't have time for slackers. If you don't work hard, you will be punished."

He went along the line, looking at each of us. Most of the men looked down at the ground and didn't meet his eyes. But King Andrew stared straight back at him.

I wanted to warn him that in this place he wasn't a king any more. He didn't have soldiers and servants at his command. Instead he was a slave, the lowest of the low.

"Keep an eye on that one. He looks like a troublemaker," the manager told the guards. Then he turned back to us.

"Perhaps you don't like this place. Perhaps you're already wondering how you can get away from here. Well, I can tell you, it's not impossible to get out of the mine – a few slaves have done it. But they didn't get very far."

He dragged one of the men out of the line by his collar. "See this? It says *Property of West Durham Mine*. Everybody for miles around knows the meaning of that collar, even if they can't read. Escaped slave, that's what it means. They won't help you to get away... They'll bring you back here because they know they'll be well rewarded."

He paused for a moment. "And, when they do bring you back here, we'll make sure your life is not worth living. You'll wish you'd been killed trying to escape. So don't try it! Understood?"

Most of us nodded. Not King Andrew, though. He was still staring at the manager as if he had the power to say, *I won't permit this kind of thing to happen in my city*.

The manager noticed at once. He marched up to the king, who was three inches taller than he was. This meant King Andrew was looking down at him.

"Enough of this insolence!" the manager said sharply. "You are a slave. You must never look at your masters like that. I'm going to use you to teach the others a lesson. Guards! Give him three days and nights on the treadmill."

The guards seized the king. He didn't try to fight them off because it was pointless. There were too many of them, and they had swords and whips.

They led him towards a tall wooden wheel, twice the height of a man. There were steps inside the rim of the wheel, and a slave was treading on them as if climbing up an endless staircase, making the wheel turn. It seemed to power some kind of machine to lift water out of the mine workings.

The slave was made to get down and King Andrew was put in his place. A guard flicked him with a whip. He started walking; the wheel began to turn with a weary-sounding creak.

"That might teach him better manners," the manager said. "If there's one thing I cannot stand, it's an arrogant slave. All of you would do well to remember it."

# 9 Slavery

Rob and I were put to work filling barrows with rocks and earth. This was in a new section of the workings, where men were digging down to reach the layer of coal that lay below the surface. They used sledgehammers to break up the rocks. We loaded the broken pieces into barrows and dumped them in the old part of the pit, where the coal had already been taken out.

The working day began at first light, when a trumpet blew outside our sleeping hut. It ended when the sun went down. Apart from two breaks for meals, we were made to work throughout that time. We went back to the hut and lay down exhausted, aching in every bone of our bodies.

There were a dozen sleeping-huts with about 50 slaves in each one. At night the doors were locked, and guards with lanterns went past on patrol. But the other slaves told us that the main barrier to escape was the wire fence around the outside of the mine. There were guards there too, armed with terrifying weapons that could shoot much further than a bow, and kill with one shot.

"So it's true," Rob muttered to me. "They do have guns in Durham."

Seeing that we were new, the other slaves questioned us eagerly. Some of them were Durham men who had been enslaved as a punishment for stealing, or deserting from the army, or simply for speaking out against Sir John. They were disappointed to hear that we were from Lothian. We couldn't give them any news of their friends and families.

"What about him out there on the treadmill?" someone asked. "Is he from Lothian too?"

I said, "Yes. In fact he's—"

Just in time, Rob pinched my arm. If King Andrew didn't want people to know who he was, then we must keep our mouths shut.

"He's got to stay there for three days and nights," Rob said.

There was a gasp of horror.

"Three days! It will kill him," someone said. "I've done it just for a day and, believe me, I was glad to get down."

"What did he do to deserve that?" another slave asked.

"Nothing. The manager didn't like the look of him, that's all," said Rob. "Totally unfair!"

This made the others laugh. "Unfair?" one of them said. "Better forget you ever knew the meaning of that word. You're slaves now. The masters decide what's fair and unfair."

The treadmill had to keep going day and night to stop the lower levels of the mine from flooding. I fell asleep to the sound of its endless creaking. I woke in the night and heard a guard shouting at Andrew. "Come on, you lazy swine! You're here to work, not sleep! Get moving." A whip cracked like a pistol shot and the wheel groaned into motion again.

After two days and nights of this, he looked like death. I pushed a barrow close to the treadmill, but he didn't see me. His head was down. He leaned on the crossbar as if he would have collapsed without its support. He could hardly lift one foot after the other, and his back was criss-crossed with whip marks.

And this was the King of Lothian! He could have stayed safe in his castle, living in luxury, surrounded by people who would obey his commands. I wondered what thoughts were going through his mind right now.

Silently I prayed for him. But, in the depths of the mine, it was hard to believe in a God who loved us like a father. If he loved us, why did he let this happen? If he didn't love us, or didn't exist, then why bother to pray?

I had saved some of the bread we'd been given earlier. "Can I give my friend some food and water?" I asked the guard on duty.

"He's already had some," the guard growled. "Get on with your work, boy, unless you want to be up there instead of him."

I hurried off. But soon after, the man did give him a drink and a few moments to rest. Guards as well slaves felt some pity for Andrew. The guards were taking bets to see if he would last the three days.

He made it – just. As we got up after the third night, the guards were getting him down from the treadmill. They dragged him over to our hut and flung him on the straw bedding. He looked dazed with exhaustion. His back and feet were covered in blood. His breathing wheezed and gasped like an old man's last breath.

Rob and I wanted to stay with him, but the guards made us go to work. "Leave him. I'll send old Eddie to look after him," one of them said.

"But he's dying!" Rob said.

"No, he's a tough one. He'll survive," the guard said, with what sounded almost like admiration.

He did survive, which was partly thanks to the old slave called Eddie. Eddie cleaned Andrew's whiplash cuts and bound up his raw, blistered feet. He brought him water and, when Andrew was able to eat a little, he fed him.

"Who is that old man?" I asked one of the other slaves.

"Eddie? He's been here for years. They say he's the oldest slave in the mine – must be 50 if he's a day."

Eddie looked more like 70 than 50. He said that the dust of the mine had ruined his lungs. He couldn't walk ten yards without stopping to breathe.

"I can't work any more," he said. "In the normal way of things, they would have got rid of me long ago. But I suppose I'm useful to them. I can patch up sick and injured slaves so that they go on working."

Rob said, "What do they usually do with slaves that can't work any more?"

Eddie said, "Kill them. What else would you expect? Food costs money. They're not going to waste it on slaves that don't earn their keep." He let out a bitter-sounding laugh, which turned into a coughing fit.

"They treat us like animals," Rob said, angrily. "We've got to get out of here!"

Yes, but how? I didn't think it would be possible. As well as escaping from the mine itself, we would have to find a way to unlock our slave-collars. Otherwise we would quickly be recaptured and punished.

For the next few days, Rob was always talking about plans for escape. But then the relentless grind of work began to wear him down. The days were so long and hard. Every day was the same as the one before. Even the food was the same every day – bread for one meal, porridge for the other. There was always plenty of food to give us energy for working, but sometimes I could hardly manage to swallow it.

There were no rest days. We had to work in all kinds of weather – hot afternoons when the sweat dripped off us and wet days when the rain lashed us like whips. "If you think this is bad, just wait until wintertime," the other slaves warned us.

Each night I went to bed so tired that I was asleep almost before I knew it. And before I knew it, too, the trumpet-call shattered my sleep. I would have to get up and start another endless-seeming day of drudgery.

I knew there was no escape. This would go on for years, until I was too old and useless to work any more, and then they would kill me. I was beginning to long for that day.

# 10 Crazy

Slowly, Andrew - we never called him "King Andrew" now - got his strength back. His feet healed over and he started walking again. Old Eddie said he might never lose the scars on his back, but then most slaves carried the same marks.

He was put to work loading coal into carts to be taken away. There were horses to haul the carts up the steep track out of the mine, but often the slaves had to help by pushing from behind. This gave Andrew a chance to get quite close to the entrance gate and the fence.

"There's not much hope of escaping by way of the gate," he told Rob and me. "It's too well guarded. The fence is a possibility, though. The guards around the outside are a long way apart."

"That's because they have guns," Rob said. "They don't need to be close together."

"Yes, but if we got out at night... by burrowing under the fence, say... we could avoid them all right. Guns aren't all that accurate in the dark. We found that out when we fought off the reivers."

I thought he was being totally unrealistic. "You'd never get near the fence - the night patrols would see you. And, even if you did get out, what about your slave-collar? If people saw it, they'd bring you straight back here."

Andrew said, "What's the matter, Jamie? Don't you want to escape?"

"Of course I want to. I just don't think it's possible."

"Don't lose heart," he said. "It's because of me that you and Rob ended up here. I'm going to make sure you get out all right."

He spoke with such confidence that I wanted to believe him. I thought that, if he was still King of Lothian, he might have turned out to be a great leader of men. And even here in the mine, the other slaves respected him. They all knew him – the man who survived three days on the treadmill, never begging for mercy, never giving in.

We were in the food queue. At meal times the rules were always a bit more relaxed. The guards changed shift, and in the changeover they didn't watch us so closely. It was a good time to talk.

It was also a time when trouble could start. Everybody was hungry and tired and bad-tempered. So I wasn't surprised when a fight broke out in the queue ahead of us. Before the guards noticed, three of the slaves had pinned down a fourth one. They began to kick him in the head – he let out a scream.

"That's one of the new lot," someone said. A new intake of slaves had arrived that morning, looking shocked and frightened, just as we probably did at first.

"Who is he? What's he done to annoy Barrowby and his gang?" Rob asked.

"I heard he used to be a guard here. Barrowby recognised him. He's been waiting to get him all day."

An ex-guard who was now a slave! He wouldn't last long in this place. I felt sorry for him. He was still getting kicked; his screams had died down to a broken moaning noise.

Somebody should do something. I waited for the guards to break up the fight with their whips, but they didn't move. Barrowby's men were stamping all over the stranger's body. Why didn't anyone stop them?

*You do it. You stop them.*

I looked at Rob. I knew he was having the same thought as I was. As it said in the Book: *Do for other people what you would like them to do for you.*

But we were both afraid. Barrowby and his gang were all fired up now. They would attack us too if we said anything to annoy them. And it was only a guard after all. He probably deserved what he was getting.

Old Eddie was braver than we were. He put a hand on Barrowby's arm, but Barrowby shook him off like a dog shaking off a flea. Then Andrew stepped forward.

He said, "Hold on. Don't kick him to death – he could be useful to us."

"What?"

Barrowby, a big, bald-headed man, stopped kicking to stare at him. I thought he would hit Andrew – nobody told Barrowby what to do, except the guards of course.

"Don't kill him," Andrew said again. "It would be a terrible waste. Listen... "

He spoke quietly in Barrowby's ear. I tried to guess what he was saying by the expressions on the big man's face. First disbelief, then scorn, and then a new emotion that you seldom saw in the mines... a look of hope, almost.

"Everybody?" he said. "You're not serious."

"Every last one of us. But I'll need your help, and his too, probably."

"All right, lads, that's enough for now," Barrowby told his men. Their victim was unconscious by now. "Dump him in a hut – Eddie can sort him out. We'll finish this another time."

The men obeyed him, grumbling. Barrowby said to Andrew, "You're crazy. Mad in the head. But I'll help you if I can."

"What on earth did you say to him?" Rob whispered, when Andrew came back to his place in the line.

"Ask me later." For everyone was giving him curious looks.

That night, in a quiet corner of the hut, he told us, "I'm going to try and organise a mass breakout. I want to get every last slave out of this place. And then – if they'll follow me – we'll have an army. We will march on Durham to fight Sir John."

"Barrowby's right," I said. "You are crazy."

"Count me in," said Rob.

The ex-guard recovered consciousness the next morning. A day or two later Eddie asked Andrew to go to him. The man was eager to thank the person who had saved his life. Rob and I went too because we were interested to know how a guard could end up as a slave.

Andrew asked the man some questions; he answered as well as he could, through lips that were cut and bruised. His name was Greg. He had worked as a guard, first at the mine, then in a mill further down the valley.

"But why were you enslaved?" Andrew asked him.

"Because I helped a slave to escape. Just a kid who'd been in an accident at the mill. One of the machines chewed up her hand and arm." He shuddered at the memory. "A right mess, it was. That was always happening. They had an accident every week or so. I hated it."

Old Eddie saw by our blank looks that we didn't know what a mill might be. He told us it was a place where woollen cloth was made on huge machines, far bigger than a cottage weaving-loom and far more dangerous. Slave children were used as workers because of their small, nimble fingers, and because they could crawl around under the moving machinery.

Greg went on, "When slaves get damaged like that, they're useless at the mill. And they make the other kids jumpy. So this girl - only about 12, she was - the mill manager told me to sell her down at the docks. He said I should get a good price for her. She wasn't bad-looking apart from that maimed arm."

"But instead you helped her to escape?" Andrew said.

"Yes. I paid her way on a ship bound for Embra. Slavery's not allowed in Lothian, people say. She'd be safe there."

I wondered what had happened to her. It was true there was no slavery in Embra – it had been banned by King James, Andrew's father – but there was a lot of poverty. The girl was probably begging in the streets by now.

"How were you going to explain it to the mill manager?" Rob asked.

"I was going to say she gave me the slip and ran away. But somebody must have seen me taking her to the boat. I don't know who – Durham's full of spies. It's terrible there now. Anybody you speak to might be in the pay of Sir John. Anything you say or do could be reported."

Andrew said eagerly, "Do you think there are people in Durham who are ready for a change of rule? Would they like to see someone else in charge instead of Sir John?"

"Do you mean his son? By what I hear, Sir Giles would be just as bad, or worse. They say Sir Giles has got a young Norsewoman locked up in Durham castle. He's going to make her marry him at the Autumn Fair, whether she wants to or not."

Andrew drew in his breath. "And how long is it until the Autumn Fair?"

"Another month or so." Greg clearly thought this was an odd question.

"Then we might still get there in time," Andrew said.

"In time for what?"

"In time to rescue Valda. That's the whole reason I'm here."

Rob said to Greg, "Don't tell anyone you heard him say that, all right? People already think Andrew's crazy. We don't want to give them any more proof."

"I can keep my mouth shut," said Greg. "Don't you worry."

"As for mad," said old Eddie, "sometimes it's the so-called mad people who manage to change the world."

# 11 Fever

In the next few days, Andrew talked to Greg whenever he had the time. He was finding out as much as he could about the guards' routine - anything that might be useful for an escape attempt. Barrowby and Eddie were included in these talks, but not Rob and me.

"If the guards think there's something going on, there will be bad trouble," Andrew said to us. "The fewer people who know, the better. And you're still young... I don't want to put you at risk."

But there were risks of a different kind within the mine. Two of the new slaves had fallen sick with a fever. One morning they were so ill that not even the guards' whips could rouse them.

Eddie was sent for. But he came out of their hut straight away and shut the door. His face was pale.

"Nobody is to go in there," he said. "It looks to me like the plague."

He went to the sergeant of the guards and told him what he'd seen. "Swelling in the armpits... a rash on the skin... vomiting blood. All the signs are there. I saw the same things ten years ago, when a slave from France brought the plague here. Two hundred slaves died that year. Some of the guards caught it too."

Now we saw a strange sight. The trumpet sounded, the sergeant shouted his orders and every single guard in the mine went hurrying up the track to the entrance. We stopped working and stared after them.

"The plague... the plague... "

As the news spread, slaves too ran towards the gates. Rob, Andrew and I went with them. But the gates were locked and barred.

"You'll have to stay and take your chances," the sergeant shouted across the fence. "We have to try and contain the outbreak. We can't have it spreading outside the mine."

"It might already be too late," Rob muttered. "The guards that were trying to get the sick men to work – they could have caught the disease."

There were angry shouts from the slaves. A few shots were fired above our heads. Then the mine manager appeared beyond the fence.

"Keep on working, if you want to eat," he ordered us. "We'll be watching you. I'm going to double the guard around the outside. Anyone coming near the fence will be shot instantly."

There was more shouting. Barrowby tried to get the men to charge at the gates. "Better to get shot than die of the plague!" he yelled.

But only a few men followed him and, when one got a bullet in the leg, the others drew back. Barrowby was left on his own, with three guns aimed at him through the fence.

The manager said coldly, "What's your name, slave?"

"Barrowby, sir."

"Well, Barrowby, you seem to be a man of action. I'm putting you in charge. You will report to me each morning. Tell me how many slaves have fallen sick. Dig a pit in the old workings – make sure all the bodies are buried deep. And get the others back to work, or they'll starve."

"Yes sir."

Of course we didn't go back to work. Barrowby didn't even try to make us do that. We stood around in anxious groups, talking fearfully about what we knew of the plague. Some said it was passed on by flea bites – and our bedding crawled with fleas – or by the poisoned breath of sick people. There was no known cure for it. If you caught it, the chances were that you would die in great pain, your skin turning black, your fingers rotting with gangrene.

I wanted to ask Eddie about what had happened last time. I found him in a hidden corner behind the huts; he told me to keep away. "I might have the sickness by now," he said.

By next morning the two sick men were dead. On the manager's orders, the hut where their bodies lay was burned to the ground. No one else was ill yet, but we were all hungry enough to start work again. The guards threw some bread over the fence that evening, and men fought over it, until Barrowby and Andrew stopped them.

Andrew made sure that Eddie, Rob and I got our share of the bread. "Come on, eat," he said to me. "Don't look so downhearted, Jamie. This plague thing could actually help us."

"How?"

"You'll find out tonight."

In the hut that night he revealed his plan.

"We're going to tell the manager that the plague is spreading. Barrowby will report each day that more men are ill and dying. After a few days, when the guards think we're far too weak to try anything, we're going to break out of here. Are you with me?"

Some slaves laughed at him. Others were quick to see the possibilities.

"More and more of us would have to hide indoors each day."

"We could pretend to bury people. The guards won't be able to see us properly from beyond the fence."

"If we break out on a moonless night, their guns won't be much use to them. We'll fight them hand-to-hand – we can take them!"

A great excitement was spreading and growing. Men who had lost all hope began to see a reason for living. Maybe, after all, they wouldn't have to die as slaves.

Andrew and Barrowby went from hut to hut in the darkness – there were no night patrols now – explaining their plans. They came back in triumph. "Almost everybody agreed to go along with it," said Andrew.

"Even if they didn't think it would work, most of them said it was worth a try."

"It'll work all right," said Barrowby. "Providing the plague doesn't mess things up."

But amazingly, no one fell ill, not even Eddie. "That is like a miracle," he said. "God is good."

Rob and I looked at him, surprised. I'd never heard him mention the name of God before. "Do you believe in God, then?" I asked him.

"Yes," he said. "In fact I used to be a preacher, long ago. But men don't want to hear the name of God in this place, and can you blame them?"

Rob asked him why he was sent here.

"Twenty years ago, Sir John banned people from owning books of any kind. Especially the Bible – he hated it. The Bible is a book of God's words to men... "

"We know. There's one in Embra," I said.

"Then you'll understand how important it is. Without it, faith in God can wither away like a dead leaf."

He stopped speaking because he'd run out of breath. The dust of the mine had made his lungs so bad that he couldn't even talk for long at a time.

After a few wheezing breaths, he went on. "Our church Bible was taken from us, but I still used to preach using the words I remembered. Then I was arrested. One of the people listening must have informed on me."

"That's terrible," said Rob.

"I never knew there were people in Durham who believed in God," I said.

"Maybe there aren't any more," said Eddie. "This happened 20 years ago."

"You've done 20 years in the mine?"

"Yes, and for most of that time I wondered why God was keeping me alive. But I knew there must be a reason... "

I looked at him with new respect. Suddenly I remembered those words that Annie had read from the Book. *If one of you wants to be great, he must be the servant of the rest...* Eddie, servant of slaves, would surely be great in God's kingdom.

Suddenly the door burst open, making us jump. But it was only Barrowby, looking excited.

"Hey!" he cried. "You'll never guess what just happened!"

He looked around the hut. Although it was time for work, the place was still half-full of slaves. During daylight hours we had to stay hidden because we were supposed to be ill or dead.

"I made my report to the boss," he said. "I told him we buried 22 slaves yesterday, and at least 30 more had fallen sick in the night. He said what did we do with the slave-collars? They cost five pounds each, he said. And from now on I have orders to remove the collars from all slaves before we bury them. Look! He gave me a key!"

As the meaning of this sank in, men scrambled over each other to get to him. He began to unlock the hated collars. Some had been worn so long that they had rusted solid, but most of them came off all right.

When it was my turn, I held my breath. With a click the collar unlocked and fell away. And somehow, although still a prisoner, I didn't feel so much like a slave.

Rob said, "There's a pale ring in the black dust around your neck. I suppose I'll be just the same."

"I wish we could wash off the coal dust," I said.

"Don't even try," Barrowby said. "That black dust will help to hide you in the darkness. We'll make our escape the next chance we get... the very next moonless night."

# 12 The Fence

The night was black as coal, wet as a waterfall. It couldn't have been better.

With no patrols inside the mine, and no locked doors, everything so far had been easy. We had climbed up the slippery slope at the eastern side of the pit. Now we lay flat on our faces at the top, not far from the fence. There were 150 men here, and three more groups were in position to the north, south and west.

Hours ago, when darkness fell, the guards had hung lanterns at various places along the fence. But it was midnight so many of the lights had burned out by now, and nobody had gone out in the rain to replace them. Ahead of us was a long, unlit stretch of fence. I could just make out a dim movement at the base of it, where four slaves were digging out a shallow trench so that we could crawl underneath.

If a patrol came past on the outside, the men would be spotted at once. But Greg had laughed at the thought. "Patrols? On a night like this? They'll be sitting in the guard posts, keeping dry."

All the same, I couldn't help remembering what the manager had said. "Anyone coming near the fence will be shot instantly... " Fear twisted my stomach into a tight knot.

God, help us... God, help us... Don't let them see us...

The man to the right of me had started moving forward. Now it was my turn to crawl towards the wire fence. In one hand I gripped the pickaxe I'd chosen as a weapon. Rob was close behind me.

It was raining so hard that the trench below the wire had become a puddle. I slithered through, feeling the sharp metal scratch the skin on my back. But it couldn't stop me - couldn't hold me. I was free!

Scrambling out of the hole, I leapt to my feet, but one of the other slaves pulled me down on the ground again. "Stay down," he hissed. "You're not safe yet - nowhere near."

Andrew was by the fence, counting as the men came through. The last of our group was old Eddie, gasping for breath.

"Don't wait for me," he whispered. "I'll only slow the rest of you down."

"No," said Andrew. "Nobody gets left behind. Rob and Jamie - I want you to look after Eddie."

Willingly we helped him up. He'd spent years looking after other people. It was his turn now to be looked after, and he leaned on our shoulders as we set off into the darkness.

The plan was to make for the road that ran down the valley towards Durham. We would meet with the other groups there - safety in numbers, as Barrowby said. If the guards pursued us, they would have better weapons, but we would easily outnumber them.

We had only gone a few paces when we heard the sound we dreaded – gunfire. It came from a distance, from the south side of the mine.

The sound alerted the guards at a nearby post. A door opened and half-a-dozen guards came out hurriedly, guns at the ready. We saw them in the light that spilled out through the doorway. The darkness still hid us, but they were coming our way. They would run right into us!

Andrew said quietly, "Get ready to attack. Nobody move until I say."

Every man obeyed him. No one made a run for it. No one panicked and attacked too soon. When the guards were almost on top of us, Andrew shouted "Now!"

The guards were taken completely by surprise. Their guns couldn't save them. They hardly fired a shot before the slaves overwhelmed them like a huge, dark wave of the sea.

Even when all the guards were dead, some of the slaves still hacked and pounded at their bodies. They'd been treated cruelly for years... now they wanted revenge.

"Come on, lads, stop that." Andrew looked taken aback by the violence and hatred he'd let loose. "You're wasting time. Our friends on the south side need our help."

"Yes!" someone shouted. "More guards. Bring on more guards!"

Andrew led the group away around the edge of the mine, heading for the place where guns were still firing. We followed them at Eddie's slow pace. Before we got there the guns fell silent, and the triumphant slaves swept on towards the next guard post.

By dawn there wasn't a single guard left alive. Most of their bodies were hacked to pieces and their skulls bashed in like broken rocks. Even a hard man like Barrowby looked sickened by this.

A dozen slaves had been shot dead, and a few more were wounded. That left over 500 men, fired up with freedom and victory and blood, eager for more action. As the dawn was breaking, they surrounded Andrew and Barrowby – a great crowd of noisy, wild-eyed, mud-stained men.

"It's not over yet," Andrew shouted. He climbed onto a coal cart, where he could see every face in the crowd. "We could tell you all to go home, but instead we want volunteers for one more fight."

"Yes!" the men roared.

"Who's the enemy?" somebody yelled.

"Sir John of Durham," Andrew said. "He's made himself rich from our slavery. And, if we don't defeat him, our freedom won't last. He could order us to be arrested tomorrow and enslaved again. So we're going to get rid of him and make Durham a better place!"

"And I suppose you want to rule instead of him," a slave called out.

"Why would I want that?" Andrew looked surprised. "I already have a kingdom of my own. I am King Andrew of Lothian."

There was a shout of laughter.

"Yes, and I'm the Emperor of Russia!"

"I always said he was crazy. Now do you believe me?"

"Come on then, crazy lad!" Barrowby shouted. "Take us to Durham!"

Soon we were marching down the valley. The wounded men, along with old Eddie, rode on coal carts. The rest of us were on foot, some carrying swords taken from the dead guards. "Leave the guns," Andrew had ordered. "They're dangerous unless you are trained to use them."

The road took us past a high-walled building with a huge chimney spewing out foul black smoke. I could hear the sound of machinery pounding away. It was loud enough out here – it must be deafening indoors.

There were a couple of guards at the gate, but when they saw us coming, they made a quick retreat.

Greg came hurrying through the crowd to plead with Andrew. "Can't we set free the slaves at the mills?"

"We don't have time," Barrowby said. "Everything depends on taking Durham by surprise."

Andrew frowned. "We will set them free when we defeat Sir John, I promise you," he said.

"What if we don't defeat him?" Greg said. "Then they'll never be free. This could be their only chance."

"All right then. You do it," said Andrew. "Take 20 men with you – we can't spare more. Catch up with us as soon as you can."

I wished I could have stayed to see the slave children released. But Andrew led us on down the valley, past rows of blackened houses, an abandoned coal pit, another mill...

The air was grey with smoke, making it hard to see into the distance. "When will we get to Durham?" I asked one of the men.

"This *is* Durham," he said, grinning. "The outskirts, anyway."

"But isn't there a city wall or a gate or anything?"

"You'll see plenty of walls and gates at the castle. Sir John keeps on building it bigger and stronger."

"The castle! Aye, that'll be a tough nut to crack," said another man.

"Nobody can stop us now," his friend said, confidently.

And so far no one had even tried, although there were people about in the streets by now. They stared at us, open-mouthed. A few of them scanned the faces of the freed slaves, as if they longed to see someone they knew.

"Come and join us!" Andrew shouted. "Fight for freedom – down with Sir John!"

Most of them looked frightened at the thought. "You haven't a chance," a man shouted. "It'll be guns against sledgehammers. Not a chance, lads."

"Down with Sir John! Down with Sir John!" the men began to chant, drowning his voice.

But soon Andrew and Barrowby told them to be quiet. "We don't want to warn them we're coming," Andrew said. "Our only chance is to surprise them."

"And we're nearly there now," said Barrowby, "so be ready."

# 13 Through the gates

The castle stood on a hill, with a river looping around it. We split into two groups to cross two separate bridges. The two groups were to meet at the main gate of the castle. Greg had told Andrew that in daylight hours the gates would probably be open, although there would be soldiers on guard.

The weather was still helping us – or not so much the weather as the smoky atmosphere. It was a man-made fog hanging over the city. The castle towers were shrouded in it. As we crossed the bridge, it covered us like a cloak.

On the other side we broke into a run, charging up a cobbled street between houses. It opened out suddenly into a wide square, with the castle looming up on one side. And the gates were open! With a wild yell we raced towards them.

It took the guards a moment to realise what was happening. Then one sounded a horn – a signal of danger – and the others started trying to close the heavy gates.

Too late... Our foremost men pressed into the gateway like a herd of stampeding cattle. They pushed the gates back, crushing the defenders against the wall.

Gunfire sounded from the castle walls. The man in front of me cried out and fell. I couldn't stop to help him.

The crowd behind was pushing me on through the gateway.

We came out into a broad courtyard. Opposite us was another arched gateway. The guards here were better prepared, warned by the signal. Already a huge portcullis gate was dropping down to close the gap.

"Quick! Follow me!" Andrew yelled.

He would have tried to dive beneath the gate, but Barrowby grabbed his arm and held him back. The gate dropped down with an earth-shaking thud.

"Don't get carried away, lad," said Barrowby. "You can't defeat Sir John single-handed. Safety in numbers, remember?"

Despite the guns firing from the inner battlements, our men took possession of the outer gatehouse and courtyard. On Barrowby's advice, they closed the gate. He was afraid of more surprise attacks from outside.

"Now what?" he said to Andrew. "Do we build a battering-ram, or sit here and starve Sir John out?"

"I don't know," said Andrew. "Why don't we see what Sir John has to say?"

We were still by the inner portcullis. This was the safest place to be, close to the wall where the soldiers above couldn't shoot at us. Andrew hammered on the gatepost.

"We demand to speak to Sir John of Durham!" he shouted.

"He's not here," someone shouted back.

Andrew and Barrowby looked at each other, taken aback. Andrew said, "We'll talk to your commanding officer, then. Ask him to come to the gate."

The officer arrived very quickly. He stood inside the bars of the gate, with Andrew on the outside. It was a dangerous situation for both of them. A spear from our side or a bullet from the other side would have ended the discussion at once.

The officer said that Sir John had ridden out that morning to inspect the harbour defences. And, when he returned, his anger would be terrible.

"Get out while you still have the chance," he said. "If you're still here when he comes back, you'll be trapped here. Caught between a rock and a hard place. You'll get shot to pieces."

"And what about you, captain?" Andrew said. "You should be afraid of Sir John's anger, too. You've allowed his gates to be invaded. You'll probably be sent to the mines as a slave – if you're lucky."

Barrowby said, "Why don't you join forces with us? If we defeat Sir John, we'll abolish slavery forever! The people of Durham won't have to live in fear any more!"

"Yes, join us!" Andrew urged him.

"My allegiance is to Sir John," the man said, stiffly. "I've served him for 15 years. I will not betray him now!"

"Your loyalty does you great credit," said Andrew. "Do you think Sir John will be as loyal to you, if you anger him?"

"Sir John is a ruthless man," said Barrowby. "But then you know that as well as we do, captain."

Suddenly we heard shouting at the outer gate. One of our men called to Andrew from across the courtyard.

"There's a crowd of people outside in the square. They've heard about us. They're looking for missing husbands and brothers and friends. Can we let them in?"

"They'll be taking their lives in their hands," said Andrew. He turned back to the soldier behind the gate. "Captain, can I ask you for a truce? Tell your soldiers to hold their fire for an hour and I guarantee my men will treat them fairly if we win this fight."

The officer agreed to this. He shook hands on it with Andrew through the bars of the portcullis.

"Do you trust him?" I whispered to Rob. "I wouldn't."

"Andrew's not stupid," said Rob. "The soldiers are Durham men. They won't want to gun down their own people."

The outer gates were opened. Into the courtyard spilled a crowd of people – men, women and children, respectable townsfolk of Durham. They ran towards our band of ragged, filthy, coal-blackened men.

How would they ever recognise each other? Somehow, some of them did. There were screams of joy from the women, and tears from children. Not only from children... strong men wept as they were reunited with the families they hadn't seen for years.

But some didn't find the people they longed for. The men might have died years ago, killed by Sir John's men or worn down by the drudgery at the mine. The families might not yet have arrived, although more and more people were pouring in through the gates.

And Andrew, too, was looking in vain for someone. He'd climbed a staircase to the top of the outer wall, and now he was gazing up at the smoke-wreathed towers of the castle. Of course – he was wondering if Valda was in there. I'd almost forgotten about Valda. But now I realised that she had never been far from his mind.

All at once I heard a horn blowing from the castle keep. The warning signal! I ran up the steps to look out over the wall.

A troop of soldiers was riding across the square. At their head rode a small, middle-aged man in a purple cloak. When he saw the people crowding in through the castle gateway, he looked furious.

Was this Sir John? Somehow I'd expected someone much bigger and fiercer-looking. But his soldiers were fierce enough, laying about the crowd with horse-whips to clear a path through the crowd.

"Andrew! Tell the men to shut the gates!" I said urgently.

"Why would I do that?" he said, calmly. "I've been waiting for a long time to meet Sir John."

The horses' hooves rang hollow through the gatehouse. I counted 20 riders as they came out into the courtyard. They carried swords and pistols. We were more than a match for 20 soldiers, but there must be many more inside the castle, ready to come to their rescue.

"Where are the guards?" roared their leader. "I'll have them whipped for this! Get this rabble out of here!"

"Are you Sir John of Durham?" Andrew shouted from the wall.

The man turned to stare up at him. "I am indeed. And you, I can see, are a slave from the mines. There's only one way to deal with scum like you. Shoot him down!"

As the soldiers drew their pistols, there was a howl of fury from our men. For the first time, Sir John seemed to realise just how many slaves were mingled with the crowd. And now they were gathering around him and his troops – dozens, hundreds of angry men.

He looked towards the inner gateway of the castle. The portcullis was still shut. A line of soldiers with guns stood on the battlements, staring down.

"What are you waiting for?" he yelled up at them. "Open fire, men! Shoot the lot of them!"

Up on the battlements nobody moved. The horsemen in the courtyard began firing wildly at the crowd. People screamed and tried to run. Horses reared up and trampled on fallen bodies.

But the slaves pressed closer, grim and purposeful. The soldiers were dragged from their horses. Sir John himself was pulled down, but he slashed with his sword and fought through as far as the portcullis.

"Open up! Let me in!" he shouted, desperately.

"Stand back, lads. He's mine," Barrowby yelled, and swung his sledgehammer.

This was how Sir John died at the gates of his own castle... trapped between a rock and a hard place, as they say. And his son, Sir Giles, was dead too. He had been one of the riders in the courtyard. In the chaos of the fight, a bullet took him in the heart.

As old Eddie said later on, "Those who live by the sword, die by the sword."

"Aye," said Barrowby. "Or by the gun. Or the sledgehammer."

# 14 Two shocks

"I kept my word," the captain of the guard said to Andrew. "I gave you an hour of cease-fire. Now will you keep your promise to me and my men?"

"Of course I will," said Andrew. "But it would be wise not to open that gate just yet. Wait till things have calmed down a bit."

For the courtyard was far from calm. Injured men crying out as their wounds were treated... a woman shrieking because her child had been shot... angry slaves still chanting, "Down with Sir John!" And all the time, more and more people were coming in from the town, adding to the noise and confusion.

"I have a favour to ask you," Andrew said to the captain. "Set free the Norsewoman called Valda, who was engaged to marry Sir Giles. He's dead now. There is no need to keep her here."

"I'll have her brought down to the gate," the captain said, and he saluted, as if Andrew was now the lord of Durham.

"I wonder if she'll recognise Andrew," Rob said. "He doesn't look much like a king these days." Like all of us, Andrew was dressed in filthy, ragged clothes. His skin was black with coal-dust, apart from the mark of the slave-collar still white around his neck.

Soon Valda was gazing out through the bars of the gate. She looked frightened. Her beautiful face was pale, like a plant kept away from the sun for too long.

Rob was right. She had no idea who Andrew was – until he spoke to her.

"Valda. Are you all right?" was all he said. But she knew his voice.

"Andrew!" she cried. "Oh, Andrew! What have they done to you?"

Her hand reached out through the bars to him, and he grasped it as if he never wanted to let it go.

"You're free now, Valda. You can go home, if that's what you want. I'll find a ship that will take you there."

"But I thought... " Her voice trailed off into silence. She gazed up at him with those intense blue eyes.

"You thought I still loved you? You were right," he said. "I'll always love you, Valda. But I don't want you to feel trapped into another marriage with a man you don't love."

For a long moment she said nothing. I wanted to shake the girl. *Can't you see what he's done for you? He gave up everything, risked his life for you...*

"Not trapped," she said at last. "Because I love you, Andrew. And I am sorry that I left you."

He drew a long breath. "Valda, will you marry me?"

"Yes. I will marry you, Andrew." Her smile was like the sun coming out.

Two days later they were married in the castle square, exchanging promises in front of what seemed like half of Durham. Afterwards there was a great feast. Many people came up to Andrew to thank him for freeing the slaves – and more than that, for freeing the city. The whole atmosphere seemed different now. People could speak their minds without fear.

Some of the freed slaves went home with their families. But others had been captured far away – Scotland, Eire, or even France. Andrew told them that, if they wanted to go back, he would try to arrange it. Sir John had been immensely rich. It was only fair that some of his gold should be used to pay for the slaves to go home.

As for the slave children from the mills, many of them were orphans. Others had been captured by the Norsemen and had no idea how to go home again – if their homes still existed. We would have to find families who would look after them.

The captain of the guard was now taking orders from Andrew. His keys unlocked many rooms in the castle keep. As well as great wealth, we found a store of books that had been confiscated years ago. They were covered in dust and cobwebs.

Andrew looked at them with interest. "If we can't get them back to their rightful owners, I'll take some of them back to Embra when I go," he said.

"What do you mean?" The captain sounded dismayed. "You're not planning to leave, are you?"

"Not right away. There are a lot of things to sort out first."

"But who will rule Durham when you've gone? A city like this needs a strong leader," the captain said.

"I was planning to give that honour to Barrowby. He's quite strong enough," said Andrew. "As long as he remembers that *strong* doesn't have to mean *harsh* or *cruel*, he'll be a good lord of Durham, I think."

Rob and I were looking at the books. "There's one here that old Eddie would be glad to have," I said. Even though I couldn't read, I could see from the cross on the front that the book was a Bible.

"Give it to him, then," said Andrew. "It's time for all this hidden knowledge to come out into the daylight."

Each day after that, old Eddie stood in front of a broken ruin opposite the castle. (In the Old Times the building had been a great church, he told us. But it was already half-ruined when Sir John came to power, and most of the stones had been used by Sir John's men to build new walls for the castle.)

Eddie read aloud from the book to anyone who would listen. His voice, freed from the dust and grit of the mine, was growing stronger. His breathing didn't sound so laboured. He was back doing the work he used to love – spreading God's good news.

Some people stopped for a while to hear him. Others just laughed and walked on. But at least there was no danger now of being arrested.

"Are you afraid of dying?" he cried. "The fear of death is like slavery. You are helpless to escape from it. You know that one day you will die and go into the darkness.

"But you don't have to be a slave! All you have to do is believe in Jesus, the Son of God. He came from Heaven and lived as a man, and he died a cruel death. Then God brought him to life again, breaking the power of death, setting us free!

"If you trust him and follow him, your name will be written in his Book of Life. Then, after you die, you can live forever, and know God's love, and see his glory.

"But it's your choice. The slaves in the mine could have chosen not to follow Andrew, who was ready to lead them to freedom. And where would they be then? They would still be slaves.

"So choose to follow Jesus. Choose freedom! Choose life!"

There was a sudden commotion in the square. A rider was spurring his horse towards the castle. It looked as if he was bringing urgent news. We ran to find out what was going on.

Andrew was coming out of the gate as the rider slid from his horse.

"Sir, four unknown ships are sailing into harbour," the messenger said. "They look like warships, but they're flying no flags except a white flag of truce. What are your orders?"

Andrew said, "Put the shore defences on full alert. Let the ships anchor. Don't fire on them unless they fire first. We must remember that they'll be expecting Sir John still to be the lord of Durham. You've no idea where these ships come from?"

"I'd say they look like warships from Lothian," the messenger said.

"If that's true, then we have nothing to fear," Andrew said, smiling. "I'll come down to the harbour myself and meet with their captains."

We followed him down the hill to the broad river estuary where the harbour lay. Four great sailing ships were coming in on the tide. The leading one looked to me like the *Dolphin*, Admiral Crawford's ship. But why wasn't the flag of Lothian flying at the masthead?

The ships dropped anchor. A rowing-boat put out from one of them. As it drew closer to the harbour wall, I saw that Admiral Crawford himself was on board.

Rob said to Andrew, "This could be a bit of a shock to the admiral. In Embra they probably think you're dead. Remember, you disappeared into a flooded river months ago."

"That's a very good point," said Andrew. "I'll wait until Crawford comes ashore before I say hello."

The admiral climbed out of the boat and stood on the quayside. To the nearest soldier he said, "I want to speak to the lord of Durham."

"That would be me," said Andrew, stepping forward. "It's good to see you, Admiral Crawford."

By this time, of course, Andrew looked more like his old self, well-dressed and clean-shaven. The admiral knew him at once, but clearly couldn't believe what he was seeing. He took a step backwards.

"Your majesty!" His face was white with shock. "They told us you were dead!"

"They were wrong then, as you see. But what are you doing here? You're a long way from home."

"Home? We have no home any more," the admiral said, bitterly. "We left Embra because we refused to serve Sir Kenneth... or King Kenneth, as he calls himself."

Now it was Andrew's turn to be struck dumb with shock.

"Your throne has been stolen from you," the admiral said. "The traitor, Sir Kenneth, attacked Embra with the Norse raiders to back him. Embra harbour is full of longships now, and the Norsemen are sitting at ease in your castle, drinking Sir Kenneth's health."

# 15 King Kenneth

We had a friend – a girl called Ali – who was a cabin hand on board the *Dolphin*. She came ashore later that day.

"I can't believe this!" she said. "They told us King Andrew was dead! And, as for you two – I kept wondering what had happened to you. The last time I saw you, you were heading for the border lands with a load of cattle. Tell me what happened."

"First of all, tell us about Embra," Rob said. "Is it true that the Norse raiders have taken the city?"

"Yes." Suddenly she looked serious and I remembered that her family lived in Embra.

"How?" Rob demanded. "Embra was well defended. How did they do it?"

Ali said, "I don't know exactly how it happened because we were at sea. We'd been lying off the coast of Durham, waiting for a signal to come ashore to pick up Lieutenant Fairfax and his men. But the signal never came. And then we got orders by radio to come back to Embra at once. The message was urgent – after that the radio cut out."

"So you sailed back?" I said.

"Yes. And we could see that something was wrong on the far side of the Forth. There was a huge column of

93

smoke going up. It looked as if Dunfermline town was burning.

"But we had our orders. We sailed into Embra harbour. Everything seemed normal at first, and the admiral went ashore to make his report. Suddenly we were surrounded by about 20 Norse longships. They'd been lying in wait around the back of Arthur's Isle."

"Didn't you try to fight them off?" I asked.

"Of course we tried! There were just too many of them. They boarded us and overran the ship. They took our weapons and gunpowder. And then the admiral came back with Sir Kenneth. He said, "King Andrew is dead. Long live King Kenneth, the new ruler of Lothian!" It sounded as if he was about to choke on the words."

"I don't understand," said Rob. "How could the Norsemen invade Embra? There were cannon defending the harbour. There were warships supposed to be patrolling the coast."

"The Norsemen could never have done it without Sir Kenneth," said Ali. "He knew all about the city's defences – he helped to create them. And he had friends in Embra, don't forget, from the time when he was in power. He was always good at persuading and bribing people. But he hasn't got many friends left now."

"Only the Norsemen," I said, angrily.

"They're not his friends," she said. "They made use of him to get into Embra. They're letting him call himself king, but he has no real power. Soon they'll get tired of

94

him, and that will be the end of King Kenneth. And the Norsemen will rule Lothian." She shivered at the thought.

"Was it the Norsemen who set fire to Dunfermline?" asked Rob.

"Yes. They started demanding money from each town along the coast. Protection money, they called it. The people of Dunfermline wouldn't pay, so the Norsemen made an example out of them."

All three of us were silent for a moment. Ruin, fire and destruction – the Norse raiders loved them. Ruin, fire and destruction might soon engulf Embra too.

"How did you get away from the city?" I asked.

Ali said, "The admiral pretended to agree with everything Sir Kenneth said. After a week or two, Sir Kenneth trusted him completely. And then one night, when the wind and the tides were right, we slipped out of the harbour... the *Dolphin*, the *Golden Eagle*, the *Typhoon* and the *Shark*. I don't know if the Norse ships tried to follow us. With the wind behind us, they could never catch us."

Rob asked why the ships had come to Durham.

"To get some gunpowder on board – the Norsemen took it all – and to warn people what's happening. If the Norsemen hold onto Embra, it won't be long before they start raiding all down this coast. The admiral thought that the lord of Durham might help to drive them out."

"I think the admiral could be right," I said.

Andrew wasted no time. He called for volunteers to sail with him to Embra and drive out the Norse raiders. An amazing number of people came forward – not only the freed slaves, but also soldiers, fishermen, sailors and townspeople.

Some were driven by fear of what would happen if the Norsemen raided Durham. Others felt grateful to Andrew for ending the cruel reign of Sir John. As for the ex-slaves, most of us would have followed Andrew to the ends of the earth.

He chose 1,000 men – the maximum that could be carried on the four warships – and equipped them from Sir John's armoury. The ships were re-supplied with weapons and gunpowder. It was all done as quickly as possible, for the winter storms were coming. Soon it would be too dangerous to put to sea.

"Why don't you wait until spring?" Barrowby asked Andrew.

"Because there might be nothing left of Embra by then," Andrew said, grimly.

Barrowby wanted to come with us, but Andrew told him he was needed in Durham. "You want to fight the Norsemen? If I lose this war, you'll have them at your gate soon enough," he said. "Stay here and strengthen the city's defences. And look after Valda."

Valda, too, had begged to go with him, but he wouldn't let her take the risk. "Stay here, where I know you'll be safe," he said. "I'll send for you just as soon as I can. If I take you with me, how can I tell the other men they have to leave their wives? I can't have one rule for me and another for my men."

On the day we set sail, I expected to see her at the quayside with all the other anxious women who were putting on a brave face to wave goodbye. Some had only just found their men again after years of separation. Now they might be losing them forever.

But Valda wasn't there. Andrew said she was ill, too ill to leave the castle. I caught him looking in that direction more than once. They had been married for such a short time, and now he was leaving her behind. I wondered if she was angry with him.

He made a brave speech, and everybody cheered. Then the anchors were raised. We sailed downriver, and I looked at Durham for the last time.

We were leaving it a better place than we'd found it. Barrowby had great plans for the city. There was to be no more slavery and no more children toiling in the mills. If men chose to work in the mines, they would be well paid and well treated, working decent hours. As Andrew said, Barrowby would be a good ruler because he had been a slave.

Old Eddie had plans too. "I'll carry on preaching as long as God gives me the breath to do it," he said. And people had begun to listen to his message – the message of life from God, life everlasting.

There was hope for the future of Durham then. But what about Embra? A thousand men and four ships... would they be enough to save a city?

# 16 Spies

The following day a storm was threatening. We took shelter in the nearest port, which was a town called Berwick, close to the border of Lothian. It was full of refugees from Embra – people who had owned a boat or the money to buy one and escape. They had managed to flee from the city after Sir Kenneth and the Norsemen took over.

Ali went looking eagerly for her family, but without success. "I don't think my parents would leave the city unless it was on fire around them," she said. "All their money is tied up in that clothes shop."

Andrew went to meet Sir Michael, the lord of the city, who was very glad to see him. He promised Andrew another 200 men to join our forces. There wouldn't be room for them on-board ship, but Andrew had already been planning to split his forces and make a two-pronged attack. Some men would stay on board under the admiral's command. The rest would march overland to Embra.

None of this could begin until the storm had passed over. Meanwhile, Andrew sent Rob and me out to question the refugees. How many Norsemen were in Embra, and how many ships? Who was manning the defences of the city – Norsemen or soldiers of Lothian? What kind of warning systems did Sir Kenneth have?

We got wildly varying answers. Most people had been too terrified to take in what was happening. The best information came from a retired soldier called Dougie. But it was three weeks since he had left Embra and, as he said, a lot could have changed in three weeks.

We took him to Andrew and the admiral, who questioned him all over again. They weighed up various possibilities. A land-based attack posed the problem of transporting our men to the islands of Embra. But an attack from the sea would be very risky. The Norsemen's strength was in their fighting ships, and they would be backed by the big guns guarding the harbour.

"You think the gun crews would fire at us?" Andrew said. "They would fight for Sir Kenneth rather than for me?"

"They think you're dead, your majesty," the admiral reminded him. "If they knew you were still the rightful king of Lothian, I have no doubt their loyalties would be with you."

Rob spoke up. "Can't we get a few of our people into the city, to tell everybody that King Andrew's coming back?"

"Yes!" said Dougie. "I would go, sir."

"Me too," I said.

"It would be extremely dangerous," said Andrew. "And the news would be bound to reach Sir Kenneth. Then we would lose the advantage of surprise."

The admiral looked thoughtful. "How easy would it be to get a few men into Embra?" he asked Dougie.

"Not too difficult. Sir Kenneth is trying to tell people that life should carry on as normal, so there are still boats going back and forth to the mainland. But the castle is well guarded, by Norsemen as well as Lothian soldiers. At least that's how things were three weeks ago."

Andrew said, "We must send in spies. We really need up-to-date information. They could take a radio with them to report back to us."

"Not a radio," said the admiral. "We don't know if the radio station in the castle is still manned, listening for messages. My ships have been keeping strict radio silence."

"The spies would have to get into the city and out again then. Is there time to do it?"

The talks went on for hours. Finally it was decided that a small group of spies would be sent to Embra. They would ride overland – it was still too stormy for sea travel. After finding out as much as they could to help plan an attack, they would leave the city and meet up with the main army on the coast to the south-east.

Rob and I both volunteered to go. We knew the city well, and we might even be able to get into the castle where we used to work.

At first Andrew was against the idea. "You're far too young to take such a risk," he said.

"It's good that we're young," said Rob. "Nobody will suspect us."

"We could dress up as beggars," I suggested. "People don't notice beggars – they try to ignore them."

In the end it was agreed that we should go, along with Dougie and a sailor from the *Golden Eagle*, who knew a little of the Norse language. He'd learned it in his youth, he told us, when he sailed on trading ships. Joe was his name.

"How well do you speak the Norse language?" Andrew asked him.

"I wouldn't say I can speak it that well, but I can understand a fair bit. Or I used to be able to... "

He didn't sound very confident. But he was the best we could find at short notice.

Early on the following day, we met at the city gates. The Lord of Berwick had provided us with horses, spare mounts and two local men to guide us. It was still blowing a gale and there were black clouds overhead... unlucky for the start of a journey, my granny would have said, but we had to go.

I felt quite scared, but I tried not to show it as we said goodbye to King Andrew.

"If old Eddie was here, I'd get him to read some words from that book of his," he said, unexpectedly. "As it is, I'll just say, may God go with you."

And, up to now, God had gone with us, I thought to myself. Even at times when it didn't feel as if he was anywhere near... even in the depths of the mine... his hand had been over us.

We left the city and rode over a hill. A mile or so along the road, Joe reined in his horse. "Stop a moment," he said. "I've got something to ask you."

"What?" said Dougie impatiently.

He hesitated. "Truth is, I really don't know the Norse language too well. It's been years since I heard it. But I know somebody who speaks it like a native, and she wants to help us. Should we take her with us?"

"*She*? This is no trip for a woman," said Dougie.

"Who is she?" asked Rob.

"A stowaway from Durham. She hid on the gun deck of the *Golden Eagle*." He grinned. "Some of the lads found her on the first night at sea, but she persuaded them not to give her away. Want to meet her?"

"This is a daft idea," said Dougie. But he followed Joe down a path to a small cove.

A rowing-boat had been pulled up on the beach and two sailors were helping a woman to get out of it. She was wrapped in a heavy cloak that hooded her face. But already I was starting to guess...

The wind caught her hood and blew it back. Golden hair streamed out like a banner. It was Valda!

She fixed Dougie with those beautiful, huge eyes. "Let me go with you," she begged him. "It is for me that Andrew lose his country. I wish to help him to save it."

# 17 Beggars

"What do you think – should we have left her?" I asked Rob.

"I don't know." He looked ahead to where Valda was riding one of the spare horses. "Maybe she's tougher than she looks."

"Andrew would never have allowed it," I said. "I didn't think Dougie would either."

"That was before he met her. She can turn on the charm all right, can't she?"

She certainly could. It was one of the things that worried me about her. Another was the fact that she was Norse, although not from the same country as the raiding Norsemen. Also, if anything happened to her, Andrew would be totally devastated. I knew he would rather lose his kingdom forever than lose Valda – and that was dangerous.

Two days later, Embra was in sight across the water. We found a farm where our horses would be safe until we needed them. Dougie sent our guides back with strict orders not to tell anyone about Valda. Andrew must go on thinking she was safe in Durham.

We went down to the shore, to a farming market I knew from my days as a city boatman. There were still boats arriving there to pick up meat for the butchers and flour for the bakers' shops of Embra. I found a man to row us across, although he asked a high price for it.

"I have to make a living. The price of everything keeps going up," he said. "How long since you were in Embra last?"

"A few months," Rob said.

"Well, don't be surprised if you find some changes."

"What kind of changes?"

But the man wouldn't tell us anything more. He rowed us across the water in silence.

The first change we saw was in the harbour. It was full of Norse fighting ships, moored so close together that you could hardly see the water. Three ships of the royal fleet were completely hemmed in by them.

On the hillsides above, I could see some of the guns that defended the harbour. They were manned by soldiers in blue and white – soldiers of Lothian, now under Sir Kenneth's command. (I refused to think of him as King Kenneth. He had no right to that title, particularly while Andrew was alive.)

The High Street wasn't as crowded as usual. Some of the shops had been boarded up. People had a depressed look about them, and even the market traders sounded subdued.

And there were Norsemen everywhere. Tall, fierce-looking warriors, they all wore weapons – swords and axes mostly, although a few had pistols in their belts. They walked like conquerors, and people moved out of their way.

How had it come to this? Embra had been a strong, proud city, secure from attack – or so everybody thought. Surely one man couldn't bring down a city?

As darkness fell we split up, agreeing to meet the following night to share our findings. Dougie was going to stay with a friend of his, and Joe had family in Embra. I led Rob and Valda to Annie's place. I was sure she would help us if she could.

Annie welcomed us as she welcomed everybody, but her face looked worried. The huge room was crowded with homeless people. The food queue was twice its normal length. A row of sick people lay to one side – some of them were badly burned. Annie told us they'd escaped from a dockside bar, set on fire by some drunken Norsemen after a fight.

"We're living on a knife-edge," Annie said. "Sir Kenneth... I mean, *King* Kenneth isn't really in charge. But the Norse leaders aren't either. It wouldn't take much for the Norsemen to run riot."

She told us what had happened after King Andrew disappeared. Lieutenant Fairfax and his men, after a long search down river, returned to Embra with the news that King Andrew must have drowned.

The whole of Lothian was thrown into turmoil. Soon it looked as if there would be civil war between two groups, both led by strong men who wanted to rule the land.

General Macrae was one, with most of the army behind him. The other was a powerful cousin of King Andrew.

While this was going on, someone must have got news to Sir Kenneth. He still had friends who knew where he was – travelling to other lands, selling the secret of gunpowder and looking for allies. When he was told that Embra could be his for the taking, allies were easy to find.

"Like it says in the Book," said Annie, "if a kingdom is divided against itself, it will fall apart. When Sir Kenneth and his Norsemen arrived, the harbour defences were unmanned – the soldiers were outside the city, getting ready to fight for Macrae."

"What about the ships of the royal fleet?" asked Rob.

"Half of them weren't even here. And, by the time they got back, it was too late. The Norsemen were already in possession of Embra, and Kenneth had made himself king."

"Why did people let him do it?" I said, angrily.

"Well, he brought peace. He stopped the war that could have torn our country apart. But peace came at a terrible price... If only we still had King Andrew! None of this would have happened if he had stayed in Embra."

I looked at Rob, and saw he was thinking the same as I was... should we tell her?

"Annie, if we tell you something, will you promise not to breathe a word to anybody?"

She nodded.

"It's not true that King Andrew's dead. He's still alive! He's coming back!"

Next morning, Annie gave us all the help she could. She found us some ragged clothes, a crutch so that I could pretend to be lame, and some bandages for Rob's "broken" arm. As for Valda, if she was to become less noticeable, her beautiful face would somehow have to be disguised.

"I know what," said Annie. "We'll make it look as if you have leprosy, and then nobody will want to come near you."

Valda shuddered. But she allowed Annie to dab blackberry juice on her face and hands, covering them with reddish-pink blotches. Annie gave her a bell to ring as a warning: *I have leprosy, keep away.*

Then we went out to start begging and spying.

I'd never really noticed before that different spots on the High Street belonged to different beggars. When I sat down by a statue, an old man arrived and started swearing at me. I moved on to the steps by the library, but a lame woman kept staring at me as if she hated me.

"You're a fake," she hissed at me. "I saw you at Annie's last night and there was nothing the matter with you! People like you give beggars a bad name!"

I left hastily and limped up the hill, finding a place on the edge of the parade ground in front of the castle. This was the highest point on the island, apart from the castle itself. I could look out across other islands, towards the hills.

Something was worrying me. It had been easy enough for the five of us to get into Embra from the mainland. But, if Andrew brought his whole army here by land, they would need dozens of boats to reach the city.

Maybe they could wade across some of the channels at low tide. Others would be too deep or too dangerous, full of clinging mud that was impossible to wade through. How was he planning to do it?

If he used the warships as troop transports, he would be taking a huge risk. He only had four of them. One well-placed cannon shot could sink a ship and wipe out a quarter of his army.

And it wouldn't be enough just to get his men here, onto the main island of Embra. They would have to capture the castle itself – a far stronger castle than Durham. It loomed over the parade ground like a cliff. It had ranks of cannon covering all the approaches, by land or sea. The main gates were closed, with two sets of guards on duty – blue-coated soldiers on the left, Norsemen on the right.

I was starting to feel that the task was hopeless. But it would be no good telling Andrew that – he didn't know the meaning of the word. He would still try to attack, and probably get himself killed, and nothing would change...

Just then I saw a face I knew. It was Will, one of the men I had worked with on the king's boat. He went past without noticing me – it was quite true, people didn't look at beggars – and headed for the castle.

Because he was in uniform, the guards didn't stop him for more than a minute or two. A man-sized door opened in one of the huge gates, and he went in.

In King Andrew's day those massive gates had stood open, except at night. Sir Kenneth must be nervous – and he had good reason to be. But the gates wouldn't keep trouble out of the castle. Trouble was already inside.

We would never be able to capture this gatehouse like the one at Durham. But it might be possible for one man, or a few men, to get in under cover. All they needed was the right uniform.

A dangerous idea was starting to take shape in my mind. I knew that Ali's father was a tailor. Was his shop still open? Would he help us?

There was only one way to find out.

# 18 Another way

We met together at twilight by the shore, well away from the lights of the High Street. It was quiet there. The only sound was the lapping of water as the tide went out.

We all had news to report. Joe said that there were around 40 Norse ships in the harbour; this meant there must be at least 2,000 Norse warriors in Embra. Adding in the soldiers of Lothian, they would badly outnumber our army.

But Dougie had talked to some men from his old regiment. They hadn't a good word to say about their new king. Dougie was sure that they would fight for Andrew rather than Sir Kenneth, if they knew he was still alive.

Rob had been studying the problem of getting an army from the mainland to the city, and he'd come up with an idea. They could use the aqueduct.

"The aqueduct? But it's not finished yet," Dougie said, doubtfully.

"That's all to the good. It means it's not being guarded at all – they don't think it's a risk."

The aqueduct was like a long bridge with many arches, designed to bring water from the hills right into the city. We could see the unfinished end, still covered in scaffolding, on the nearest island to the south. Maybe Sir Kenneth couldn't spare the money to complete it.

If our men reached the end of the aqueduct, there would be just one more channel to cross – a shallow one which could be forded at low tide. The attack would have to be made in darkness, for the aqueduct was within range of the castle guns. But Rob was right – it was a possibility.

I told the others about my plan for getting into the castle itself. Ali's father was making a copy of the uniform that the royal boatmen wore. He didn't think it would be too difficult, apart from the hat.

Dougie was worried about my plan. "Too dangerous. If you get caught, it'll warn Sir Kenneth there's something in the wind. And what are you aiming to do, anyway?"

"I don't know yet. Find out more information? Open up the water gate to let our men in?"

"The water gate! I always said that was the castle's weak point," said Dougie. "Boatmen aren't soldiers and never will be. No discipline."

Then it was Valda's turn to speak. She had overheard an argument between two groups of Norsemen who followed different leaders. Sigurd's men were about to go on a mission, and Karl's men wanted to go too. They were all bored with sitting around in Embra – they wanted some action.

"Did they say what the mission was?" asked Dougie.

"I think it is to make a raid on... Sterling? Stirling? A big raid – 12 ships will go."

"When?"

"In three days."

This was vital news. If only Andrew could make his attack while the raid was taking place... But was there enough time to ride back to Berwick and warn him?

"I wish we had that radio machine," Rob said. "We could talk to him right now."

"There's a radio in the castle," I said. "If it's still usable... "

Suddenly everyone was staring at me.

"Do you know how to make the thing work?" asked Dougie.

"I think so." On the warship *North Star* I had helped the radio operator many times. But that was over a year ago. I just hoped I could still remember the details.

After a long talk, we came to a decision. Joe would set off for Berwick at once, taking a spare horse, and riding night and day. Meanwhile I would try to reach the radio in the castle – a quicker but much riskier thing to do.

"Don't let yourself get caught," Dougie warned me. "They mustn't start to suspect an attack. If they do, we're sunk."

Ali's father sat up all night making my uniform. It was an almost perfect copy of the one I used to wear – blue trousers and a gold-braided jacket embroidered with the royal crest. No hat though. I would have to pretend I'd lost it.

"Tell them you had a night on the town," Dougie said. He made me rinse my mouth out with whisky so that my breath would smell. I hated whisky. The taste was still burning at the back of my throat.

All alone, I set out across the parade ground towards the castle gate. Both sets of guards, soldiers and Norsemen, were watching me. I tried to look normal and unafraid, but my heart was thumping away like a drumbeat calling men to battle.

"Password?" the sergeant demanded.

I stopped in my tracks. They never used to ask for a password!

"He can't remember," jeered one of the men. "And where's his hat? Man, he must have had a good night last night."

"Password!" barked the sergeant.

"He's just a lad, sarge," said another man. "I bet it's the first time he's ever had a skinful."

"You boatmen are all the same," the sergeant muttered. "Listen, son, I'll let you off this time, but never again – understood?"

"Yes, sir."

The Norse guards meanwhile were having a good laugh at me. One of them pretended to sway drunkenly. The sergeant gave them a disgusted look.

A soldier hammered on the small door, and it was opened from the inside. I walked through the gatehouse, feeling giddy and weak at the knees. I was inside the castle!

Everything looked much as usual, apart from the Norsemen walking about as if they owned the place. I went cautiously up the hill, wary of meeting anyone I used to know. They might ask questions about my sudden reappearance.

There would be more guards at the gateway to the inner courtyard. As a boatman, I had no reason to go in there – it would look suspicious. And I didn't know the password. But I had to reach the radio room in the highest tower.

Rob, who had been a messenger, knew all the ins and outs of the castle. He had told me another way to get there without going past the guards. Down a narrow stairway and through the back door to the kitchens... along a corridor... I ducked behind a pillar when a chef went past, whistling.

More steps led me down to a huge, dim-lit cellar full of sacks and barrels. I got lost here for a few panicky minutes. At last I found my way to a door in the corner. A spiral staircase lay beyond.

This should take me up into the main buildings of the inner courtyard. But, if anyone saw me, they'd want to know why I was there, and I had no excuse at the ready.

*Oh, God, help me! You brought me safely this far. Show me the way... hide me from my enemies...*

I went softly up the stairs until I reached a door. There were voices beyond, and I let them fade into silence. Then I stepped into an empty passage. Around a corner –

another door, another spiral staircase – and suddenly I knew exactly where I was. This was the stair leading up to the radio room!

What if the door was locked? What if the machine wasn't there any more? I would have to find my way out again, and all for nothing.

But the door wasn't locked. The room looked exactly as it had a year ago, except that there was a book lying open on the table that held the radio. A chair was pushed back, as if someone had recently left the room.

Quick... be quick... they might come back at any time...

I gave a couple of turns to the handle that powered the machine. It looked all set up and ready, as far as I could tell.

"Calling the *Dolphin*. *Dolphin*, do you hear me?"

There was no answer.

I tried again. "Jamie Brown with an urgent message for the *Dolphin*. Are you receiving me?"

Still nothing, and I remembered that the admiral had ordered radio silence. Did that mean nobody was manning the machines on the ships? Or was somebody listening out there, forbidden to reply?

Then I heard footsteps coming up the stairs.

I looked around frantically. No bolt on the door. Nowhere to hide except behind the door itself. I darted behind it and took out my knife.

The footsteps were slow and uneven. Just one person, and lame, by the sound of it. A lame radio man? Surely it couldn't be...

It was. It was Graham, who had once been radio operator on the *North Star*. This was a huge piece of good fortune!

Or maybe not. It looked as if he was working for Sir Kenneth now. Be careful... be very careful...

When I stepped forward and said his name, he nearly jumped out of his skin.

"Jamie! What are you doing here?"

"I could ask you the same question. Last time I saw you, you were working in the public library. Have you got your old job back?"

"They call it my old job, but it isn't." His voice was bitter. "All I'm doing is listening out for messages between the ships of the rebel fleet. And there never are any. It's even duller than the library."

"So you work for Sir... King Kenneth?"

"Everybody works for King Kenneth," he said, wearily. "It's that or starve."

I took a quick decision, based entirely on his tone of voice.

"Well, I don't work for him," I said. "This uniform is a fake. I'm here because I have to get a message to Admiral Crawford. Will you help me?"

# 19 Send and receive

It was a good thing I had Graham to help me, for I had forgotten something vital.

"You have to turn that switch on when you send," he said, "and turn it off to receive. See?"

I tried once more. "Calling the *Dolphin*... I know you're supposed to keep radio silence, but I've got to know if I'm getting through. *Dolphin*, do you hear me? Just say yes or no."

I flipped the switch to "receive" and waited.

"Yes," came a voice, sounding faint and far away. My heart leaped.

Graham said, "The less I know about this, the better. I'll leave you to get on with it." I heard his slow footsteps retreating.

As quickly as I could, I told the radio operator everything we had found out. He asked me to stay in contact. The admiral would want to hear all this for himself.

"All right, but I may not have much time... it's dangerous here."

I listened impatiently for the admiral's voice. He would have to be brought from the upper deck to the radio room. Or maybe the ship was still at anchor and he was ashore. Oh, hurry... hurry...

Suddenly I heard another noise – feet on the stairs. More than one person, by the sound of it. A terrible fear took hold of me. Had Graham sent for the guards? Was he really on Sir Kenneth's side?

I quickly set the switch to "send". "Keep silence! They'll be listening!" I said urgently. "I repeat – don't use the radio!"

There was no way of knowing if they'd heard me at the other end. I moved swiftly behind the door as it opened.

"Where's the operator?" demanded a voice I recognised. Sir Kenneth!

He stepped into the room, followed by two other men – soldiers or bodyguards, for I could hear the clink of metal.

"I gave orders that all operators must stay here during their hours of duty," Sir Kenneth said, angrily. "It's vital that we hear any messages between the ships of the rebel fleet."

Maybe Graham hadn't said anything, after all. Maybe this was just a routine inspection, and they would go away again... please, God...

They didn't go away. They waited. I stood frozen with fear, trying not to breathe.

"The operator's coming now, your majesty," said one of the men.

Graham came up to the doorway. To make space for him, one of the guards moved further into the small room. He turned his head and saw me at once.

"Hey! Come out of there!"

The two guards grabbed me by the arms and dragged me forward to face Sir Kenneth.

I was terrified. All I could think of was that a year ago, in this very same tower, I had helped to get Sir Kenneth arrested. Would he know my face? Would he remember that day?

It seemed he didn't. Maybe I had changed – he certainly had. His face was lined; his hair was thinning. He looked much older than a year ago. Ruling Lothian must have brought him problems, not pleasures.

But he still had a commanding voice. "What do you mean by this? You are a boatman. You shouldn't even be in this part of the castle! How did you get in?"

When I didn't answer, one of the guards twisted my arm up behind my back so hard that I cried out.

"Answer or there will be worse to come," he said.

"Through the back door to the kitchens," I gasped.

Sir Kenneth frowned. "This is a serious matter," he said to his bodyguards. "He's just a youngster. But what if he'd been an assassin, sent to kill me?"

"More likely he was trying to send a message to the rebels, your majesty. Why else would he be here?"

Sir Kenneth stared at me with narrowed eyes. "Well, boy? I want an answer. What are you doing here?"

I was thinking desperately. "I just wanted to send a message. This girl I know... she's a cabin hand on the *Dolphin*. I haven't seen her since they sailed away. But the radio man wasn't here, and I didn't know how to work the machine... "

It wasn't exactly a lie, but it wasn't the truth either. Something in my face or my voice must have told him that.

"Take him away," Sir Kenneth ordered. "Find out how much truth is in this tale. Use the thumbscrews if you have to. And as for you, operator... "

As they took me down the stairs, I could hear him raging at Graham. It sounded as if Graham had lost his job again. But that was the least of my worries.

In the castle jail the guards searched me and took away my knife and belt. Then I was locked up alone in a small, cold cell. I lay down on the rock-hard bed, wondering what they would do to me.

It was a good thing Graham didn't know about our plans. But I knew everything. Would I be able to keep my mouth shut? If I couldn't, Sir Kenneth would be warned of the attack. And our men would walk straight into a trap.

When I thought of the thumbscrews, my stomach lurched. I'd seen what they could do. The previous night, Annie had been tending to the mutilated hands of a beggar. He'd been punished for theft by having all his fingers mercilessly crushed. One thing was certain – he would never pick pockets again. "King Kenneth believes in short, sharp punishments," Annie said, grimly.

I was dreading the sound of the door being opened. But nothing happened all day. I lay there, watching a patch of sunlight travel slowly across the wall. Had they forgotten about me? I really hoped so – even if that meant no food or water.

By the evening I was very thirsty. I heard a noise outside the door, and a small panel slid back at eye level, just for a few moments.

"Please could I have some water?" I asked. There was no answer. The panel slid shut.

Maybe they thought that hunger and thirst would soften me up a bit – make me ready to talk. Well, I'd been hungry plenty of times before. But thirst... that could be a real killer.

I lay down again and tried to pray. My mouth was dry and my heart was full of fear.

*Oh God, why did you let this happen? You are God – you can do anything. Couldn't you have stopped Sir Kenneth from finding me?*

Sleepless, I listened to the sounds of the night, carried in through my window on the chilly breeze. Some drunken Norsemen stumbled past, bawling out a song. An owl hooted. A dog barked far away.

Once again I prayed – desperate, hopeless prayers. *God, you said in the Book that you love me. So why is this happening to me? I'm so afraid...*

But I felt that nobody was hearing me... I was sending out a radio message with no one out there to receive it. At last I gave up and just lay there.

It was as if I'd turned the switch from "send" to "receive". When I stopped my frantic gabbling, God spoke to me.

Like a quiet voice, some words from the Book slid into my mind. Annie had read them the night before. I had only been half-listening – my thoughts had been full of our plans and schemes. But now they came back to me clearly.

*What we suffer at this present time cannot be compared at all with the glory that is going to be revealed to us.*

That meant heaven, Annie said – the glory of heaven. And we would all see it, if we believed in Jesus. If our names were written in his Book of Life, then death was nothing to be afraid of.

*Who can separate us from the love of Christ? Can trouble do it, or hardship or persecution or hunger or poverty or danger or death? ...No, in all these things we have complete victory through him who loved us.*

A great joy filled me, driving out all my fears. I felt I could float up to the ceiling. For most of that night I lay awake. I was a prisoner, hungry and thirsty, my life in danger. And yet that joyful feeling kept on welling up inside me.

It was a gift from God. It helped to strengthen me for what lay ahead.

# 20 Questioning

The door was thrown open and two guards strode in.

"You're wanted for questioning. Get up!"

They took me to an upper level of the building. I'd had nothing to eat or drink since breakfast the previous day. After climbing the stairs, I felt quite dizzy.

I felt worse when I looked around the interrogation room, with its bloodstained floor. The walls were hung with fearsome-looking metal objects. Were those what thumbscrews looked like? I turned away quickly.

I was brought before a middle-aged man in uniform. I guessed he was the governor of the jail – probably one of Sir Kenneth's friends.

"You've had a few hours to think about things. I hope you've decided that it would be wise to tell us the truth," he said. "Why did you go to the radio room?"

I said nothing because I didn't know what to do. Half-truths hadn't helped me the previous day. I didn't want to lie because lying was against God's word – and, anyway, what sort of lie could save me now? As for the true story, I would have to keep it secret for as long as I could.

The governor said, "You must know that going there was a breach of regulations. Why do you think we have guards and passwords – for the fun of it?"

When I still said nothing, he nodded to one of his men, who stepped forward and hit me full in the face. I staggered backwards.

"Why were you in the radio room?"

He asked me again and again. Each time, the guard hit me in the face or the stomach. The pain was terrible.

*Oh God, help me... oh God, help me to keep silent...*

After a while he changed tactics. "Look, I don't want to put you through this. I want to help you if I can – but you have to help me too. Tell me your name, lad."

I told him because I couldn't see what harm it would do.

"And you're one of the king's boatmen? I think we should check up on that – just in case." He sent a man to fetch the master boatman.

I had a short rest from the questioning. My head was throbbing; my nose felt as if it was broken. There was blood all down the front of my uniform. The master boatman, Dave McNab, looked shocked when he saw me.

The governor said, "This boy was discovered in the radio room, where he had no business to be. He says his name is Jamie Brown. Is he one of your boatmen?"

"He was, sir. But he left several months ago. I believe he volunteered for that ill-fated mission of King Andrew's."

"Didn't you make him turn in his uniform?"

"Of course, sir. I don't know how he got hold of another one."

The governor turned back to me. "This is a very serious offence, boy. Impersonating a member of the royal staff... entering the castle illegally... It looks to me as if you're a spy. Do you know what we do with spies?"

I started to shake my head, then stopped because it hurt too much.

"We hang them," he said. "But first we make them tell us everything they know."

More questions. Who was I working for? What was my message for the rebel fleet? Was the admiral planning an attack on the city?

When the guards kept on hitting me, Dave McNab looked horrified.

"Sir," he said, "the boy's only about 14. Surely he can't really be a spy? Maybe the reason he's saying nothing is because he knows nothing."

"Thank you, Mr McNab. You can go now."

I heard his feet hurrying down the stairs, as if he wanted to get out of there as soon as possible. That was the last thing I heard, for the dizziness was making everything swirl and sway. A merciful darkness descended on me.

When I came to, I was back in my freezing cold cell. It was dusk by now. My outer clothes felt damp, and I guessed the guards had tipped water over me, trying to revive me. But they'd failed. Probably that had saved me from more violence.

There was a small cup of water by my bed... not enough to quench my thirst, but enough to keep me alive for another day. Still no food, although I don't think I could have eaten any. Just sipping water was painful enough to my swollen mouth.

But I had managed not to give away our secret – that was the main thing. If only I could keep silence for one more day, or maybe two... Andrew's attack should have taken place by then and, win or lose, the secret wouldn't matter.

Next day I waited for the ominous rattle of keys outside my cell. I felt awful. My stomach was covered in bruises. Probably my face was, too, and I could hardly see out of one eye.

For hours, nothing happened. I switched back and forth between praying and worrying. I was desperate for news from the world outside. Had the Norsemen set out for the raid on Stirling? Was Andrew's army drawing closer to the city? What had happened to Rob and the others?

Then I was called again for questioning. This time, as I was led to the door of the upstairs room, someone else was being carried out. His face was blood-smeared and his head lolled to one side like a broken toy. I barely recognised him.

Dougie! Oh, no! How had they caught him? Had he told them anything?

"As you see, we've captured a friend of yours," said the governor. "He was found spying on the harbour defences. He's told us quite a lot about your plans. All we need is for you to fill in some details."

I didn't believe him. He was trying to trick me – he had to be. Surely Dougie wouldn't have said any more than I had?

"He told us about the rebel fleet finding refuge at Aberdeen," said another voice. I turned to look – Sir Kenneth was standing by the window. "He told us they're planning to attack Embra in three weeks. So you see, you may as well spare yourself some pain and tell us all you know."

I felt relieved. Dougie had told them a load of rubbish, by the sound of it. But what was I to say now?

There was a sudden knock at the door. It was one of the castle messenger boys.

"Your majesty, I have an urgent message from the radio room. They've picked up a signal from the *Dolphin* to the *Golden Eagle*. The rebel ships are to meet in the Firth of Tay tomorrow."

My first reaction was dismay. Hadn't the operator heard my warning not to use the radio because the enemy was listening in?

"This is bad timing," Sir Kenneth said, frowning. "Twelve Norse ships have just set out on a raid, and it's too late to recall them. But we mustn't let this opportunity go by. Take a message to Karl and Nils... Ask them to meet with me in the great hall."

Suddenly I understood why the *Dolphin* had sent that message - to draw more Norse ships out of Embra harbour on a wild goose chase. Wherever Andrew's ships might be at that moment, it certainly wasn't the Firth of Tay.

"You needn't waste any more time on the spies," Sir Kenneth told the governor. "Hang them tomorrow at midday, and make it as public as possible. I want the whole of Embra to see what happens to traitors."

# 21 Be ready

That night I kept waking up and listening. If Dougie and I were to be hanged the next day, the one thing that might save us would be an attack by Andrew's army. So I was listening for gunshots, cannon fire, shouting...

The night went slowly by. The dawn came, grey and foggy. I thought there might at least have been sunshine, if this was the last dawn I would ever see on earth.

I tried to recall those words from the Book. The words came back to me, but without the joy they had brought me before. My thoughts were as grey and chilly as the mist.

Annie had said that death was nothing to be afraid of. But how could she know? How could anybody know for sure? The dead couldn't come back to tell us what it's like.

Except for one man. One man died and was brought to life again, breaking the power of death forever. It was all written in the Book.

And he promised his friends that, when they died, they would be with him in heaven, his father's house. Very soon now, I would find out if that promise was true.

*Lord, I do believe. Help me when I start to doubt. Help me when my heart fails and my blood turns to water. I need your strength... I can't get through this on my own.*

*Forgive me for all the wrong things I've done in my life. Wash them away – make me clean and perfect, ready for heaven. Ready to see you face to face.*

The panel in the door slid back. "You've got a visitor," the guard said.

It was Dave McNab, the master boatman. He'd heard I was condemned to death, and he had come to see if I had any last wishes. The guards let him into my cell, locking the door behind him.

"Have you got any relatives that you want me to get in touch with?" he asked.

"No." They were too far away and, in any case, I didn't want them to know about this. It would only hurt them.

"Want anything to eat? Or a drink or two?"

"Just some water."

He banged on the door and made the guards pass in a jug of water. I drank it thirstily.

Dave looked pityingly at my bruised face. "They shouldn't have done this," he said. "It would never have been allowed in King Andrew's day. But nowadays things are different."

"What do you think of Sir Kenneth as king?" I asked him.

He looked nervously at the door. Nobody seemed to be watching through the panel.

"I think it was a bad day for Lothian when King Andrew died," he muttered.

For some reason I felt I could trust him, and there was something I had to say.

"He didn't die. He's coming back to Embra very soon," I whispered.

Dave stared at me, and I could guess what he was thinking – the poor young lad's been driven crazy.

"I'm not mad," I said. "I know King Andrew's still alive – I saw him less than a week ago. He's coming back at the head of an army. But they'll never take the castle unless they have help on the inside. Will you open the water gate and let them in?"

Dave said, "You've been dreaming, son. A good dream to have, though... I wish it was real."

"It's not a dream! Will you be ready?"

"All right." He smiled, as if humouring my madness. "I'll be ready."

After he'd gone, I wished I could have taken back my words. What if he told Sir Kenneth what I had said? But somehow I didn't think he would.

If only he had believed me...


The morning crawled past. I was glad I hadn't asked for food; I had a sick feeling in my stomach.

Then my cell door opened for the last time. The hour had come.

Dougie and I, our hands tied behind us, were put on a cart. Dougie was awake, but he looked in a bad way. He groaned as the cart bumped down the cobbled road to the gatehouse.

There was still a thick sea mist filling the air. It hung like a grey curtain beyond the edge of the parade ground, where the land fell steeply down to the water's edge. Most of the city was invisible. But plain to see was the gallows where they planned to hang us.

A crowd had gathered – soldiers and Norsemen, townspeople and beggars. I saw Valda, still in her leprosy disguise, with people keeping well clear of her. Rob was nowhere in sight. Maybe he could not face watching this.

Sir Kenneth sat on a throne-like chair raised up on a wooden platform. He was surrounded by armed guards. He must know that he wasn't exactly popular in Embra. As our cart came to rest beneath the gallows, he gave a grim smile.

We had to stand up on the cart. Ropes were knotted around our necks. I could guess what would happen... The cart would be pulled from under us, and we would drop down to hang in mid-air. I only had one prayer now – that it would be over quickly.

But first Sir Kenneth had to make a speech. I didn't listen beyond the first few words, for I was looking at Valda. Her eyes were fixed on my face. When she saw that she had my attention, she looked deliberately to the south, and smiled.

Somewhere out there lay the aqueduct, invisible beneath the mist. Was she trying to tell me something? Had Andrew's men already reached the city?

Then she looked back over her shoulder in the direction of the harbour. Again there was nothing to see – only fog. But I thought I could hear something... people shouting? The sound was muffled by the mist.

Sir Kenneth's speech was a short one, for the crowd was getting restless. As he drew to a close, Valda's smile turned to a look of dismay. She mouthed something at me. *We need more time*, I thought she said.

"And this is what will happen to you, if you betray your country," Sir Kenneth declared. "This is how Embra deals with traitors and spies!"

"You are a traitor also!" Valda shouted. "Yes, you, King Kenneth. You bring the Norse raiders to Embra!"

For a moment there was a shocked silence. Valda had said what nobody dared to say openly. Then a murmur of agreement ran through the crowd. Traitor... traitor...

"Arrest her," Sir Kenneth said, tight-lipped. Three soldiers moved towards Valda, but when they saw the signs of leprosy on her face, they backed away in horror. None of them wanted to touch her.

Valda scrambled up onto the cart beside me. Still shouting at Sir Kenneth, she started to free me from the noose around my neck.

"You traitor, Kenneth! You take the throne of King Andrew! You say he is dead. But he is not dead. He's alive! He is here in Embra!"

"What nonsense." Sir Kenneth's face was pale. "She's a dangerous madwoman. Kill her! Did you hear me? That's an order!"

A trumpet sounded from the castle wall. A cannon boomed, firing a warning shot above our heads. I saw a tide of men pour out of the gatehouse, and my heart sank.

But hold on – most of them weren't soldiers of Lothian. They were ex-slaves, Embra boatmen and Berwick soldiers. They were Andrew's men, with Andrew himself at the head of them. They had taken the castle!

There was only one way they could have done it so swiftly and so peaceably. Dave McNab must have believed me after all. He had opened the gate and let them in.

Sir Kenneth looked as if his worst fears had come upon him. But he was still a proud man and a fighter. He stood up on his stage and faced King Andrew over the heads of the crowd.

"Well, Andrew," he said. "This is a surprise. Where have you been hiding all this time, when your people needed you?"

"Not hiding," said Andrew. "I was captured and sold as a slave. Believe me, I came back as soon as I could. And I find that you've sold Embra to the Norse raiders."

"That's a lie. The Norsemen are our allies." As he said it, the Norsemen were gathering around him. There were not nearly as many of them as I'd feared – more than half their number must be out of the city – but they looked as if they were ready to fight for their lives.

Meanwhile, the townspeople were chanting King Andrew's name, and waving their hats in the air. Idiots! Couldn't they see that they were about to be caught up in a desperate battle? They would be massacred!

I saw a disturbance in the crowd. Rob was pushing his way through to us. He was panting as if he'd run all the way up High Street.

"The harbour's in our hands," he gasped. "There wasn't a shot fired. The gun crews have come over to our side. And our ships are on patrol to stop the raiders coming back."

This was when Valda made her great speech. It was in Norse; I had no idea what she was saying, but all the Norsemen turned to listen to her. And suddenly Andrew recognised her voice. He stared at her in disbelief.

The Norsemen started arguing among themselves. Then one of their leaders spoke up.

"The two kings must fight with swords," he said. "One dies. The other is the winner, and we follow him."

"This is what we do when two leaders quarrel," Valda explained to Dougie and me. "The leaders fight and the people are not killed. Andrew will win, of course."

"Don't be too sure," muttered Dougie. "Sir Kenneth used to be a good swordsman. It's the old fox that knows all the tricks."

"He'll never agree to fight Andrew," I said.

But it looked as if he had no choice. His soldiers were deserting him one by one, vanishing into the crowd. That left the Norsemen as his only supporters, and they were chanting one word over and over. If I had to guess, I'd say it meant, "Fight! Fight! Fight!"

"Agreed, Sir Kenneth?" said Andrew.

"Agreed. Don't forget who first taught you swordsmanship, young man." But Sir Kenneth looked ill at ease, and I didn't blame him.

There was a pause while a man was sent to fetch Sir Kenneth's sword and shield from the castle. The Norsemen started to push back the crowds so that there would be space for the fight.

Andrew seized Valda and swung her down from the cart. "Why didn't you stay safe in Durham, like I told you to?" He kissed her stained and spotted face, raising a gasp of horror from the crowd.

Sir Kenneth was standing by the wall at the edge of the parade ground. I thought he was looking out across the city. Then I remembered that it was shrouded in fog.

All at once he climbed up onto the wall, hesitated for a moment – and jumped.

# 22 All the world

Did Sir Kenneth mean to kill himself or was he trying to escape? People would argue over that for weeks to come.

If the tide had been in, the water would have broken his fall and he might have lived. As it was, his body was smashed against the rocks. He must have died instantly.

I think he knew that he couldn't win against Andrew. He was a proud man who hated to lose. And he was about to lose everything – the crown, his reputation, his life. He left behind only an evil memory, and nobody mourned him.

The Norse leaders informed King Andrew that they were on his side now. He told them that he didn't need them or want them.

"I'm grateful to you for helping me avoid a battle that would have killed many of my people. For that reason I'm giving you until nightfall to get out of here. After that, our guns will blast your ships out of the water."

They went without argument. According to Valda, they were tired of living in Embra – there was nothing to do except eat, drink and get fat. They wanted to go back to their old way of life, sailing the high seas.

When the rest of the Norse ships returned from their raid, they found Embra ready to defend itself. After several ships had been sunk by cannon fire, the others sailed away. The winter storms were beginning, and it wasn't likely that they would come back... at least, not this year.

"But we must be watchful," said King Andrew. "We must keep our country united and strong."

All through that winter I felt restless without knowing why. Everything seemed to be going well. King Andrew was proving himself to be a great king – strong, wise and fair. Valda, who had once been hated, was a heroine now. There were rumours that she was expecting a baby, an heir to the throne of Lothian.

In gratitude to Rob and me, King Andrew offered us good jobs in his service. Rob was made head of all the king's messengers. But I said I would rather stick to my old work as a royal boatman. It was a job I liked and could do well.

One day we took King Andrew out to look at the aqueduct. It was being altered and fortified so that it could never again be used as a high road into Embra.

Andrew looked up at the great arches towering over our boat. "I won't forget that march into the city," he said to me. "We took a risk, setting out under cover of the mist. If it had cleared while we were still up there, we would have been seen. The castle guns would have shot us to pieces."

"Why didn't you wait until nightfall?" I asked him.

"Something kept telling me, *don't delay*. It was like an urgent voice inside my head. I didn't know your lives were in danger... I just knew there was no time to waste."

"Maybe God was speaking to you," I ventured to say.

"Maybe," he said. "I would like to know more of this God. If old Eddie was here, I could ask him."

"There are people here in Embra who could tell you more. And there's a book – it's called the Bible. There's a copy in your own library."

"Is there? I must read it," he said.


"Do you think my life was saved for a reason?" I asked Annie. "I could easily have died that day. I was ready, and I wasn't scared."

"Weren't you?"

"Well, part of the time I wasn't scared. Part of the time I was terrified," I admitted.

"Most people would be," she said. "Jesus himself prayed that he wouldn't have to face death. He knew there was a reason for his death, and great good would come out of it. But, even so, he prayed that it wouldn't happen."

A reason for his death... a reason for my life... Was there something that God wanted me to do? If so, I wished I could know what it was. Then I might not feel so restless.

That night, Annie read out our verse of the week. It was what Jesus said to his friends, the last time he met with them on earth: *Go into all the world and preach the good news to everyone.*

"We can't all travel far away," said Annie. "*All the world* includes the place we're in right now. Our friends, our families... Have they heard the good news of Jesus? Are their names written in his Book of Life?"

I was thinking about this the next day, walking down the High Street. I had never found it easy talking to people about God. I wasn't a preacher like Eddie or an outgoing person like Annie, who could talk to anyone.

A man was coming up the hill from the harbour. I half-recognised his face, but I couldn't put a name to him. He walked past me without any sign that he knew me. That was strange, for I was sure I'd met him before.

I turned to look again. Then I knew him by the guitar slung over his shoulder.

"Sam!" I cried. "Where have you been all this time?"

He recognised my voice. But his eyes searched the crowd without picking me out. His eyes... he could see!

"Over here," I said. "It's me – Jamie."

"I always wondered what you looked like," he said, smiling. "Now I know. How are you doing?"

He told me that Annie had taken him to a doctor, who cut away a part of his eyes and made him see. This had been months earlier. He still hadn't quite got used to the huge difference it had made to his life. He'd gone travelling again, this time able to see things and walk about unaided.

"Where did you go?"

"All up the west coast on a trading ship. We stopped at every little island to trade in sheepskins and wool. And Jamie, listen to this – I met your dad! When he knew we'd sailed from Embra, he came asking if anybody had news of his boy Jamie."

"He's got no idea what a big place Embra is," I said. "Are my family all right?"

"Yes, and they were eager to hear news of you. I told them you'd gone away south on a mission for the king – that was the last I'd heard of you. And your dad said, 'Do you think he'll ever come back to us?'"

Suddenly I knew what I had to do. *Go into all the world...* for me, that meant first of all going home to Insh More.

When I told Rob this, he looked horrified. "Leave Embra? Go back to a quiet little island where nothing ever happens? Not me," he said. "You go, if you like."

Once, I wouldn't have dared to set out without Rob. He was always the leader and the fearless one. But now I could face it alone. I felt as if I had grown up a lot since I left home.

"Think of the stories we can tell them when we go back," Rob had said ages ago. And the tale of my adventures would probably fill many long winter nights.

But I had an even better story to tell my people... the story from the Book. The story that will never end. The good news of life from God – life everlasting.

143

# Great books from Scripture Union

## Fiction

A Captive in Rome, Kathy Lee  £4.99, 978 184427 088 0
The Dangerous Road, Eleanor Watkins  £4.99, 978 184427 302 7
Fire By Night, Hannah MacFarlane  £4.99, 978 184427 323 2
The Scarlet Cord, Hannah MacFarlane  £4.99, 978 184427 370 6

## The Lost Book Trilogy

The Book of Secrets, Kathy Lee  £4.99, 978 184427 342 3
The Book of Good and Evil, Kathy Lee  £4.99, 978 184427 368 3
The Book of Life, Kathy Lee  £4.99, 978 184427 369 0

## Lifepath Adventures

A Land of Broken Vows, Steve Dixon  £4.99, 978 184427 371 3
Hard Rock, Fay Sampson  £4.99, 978 184427 372 0
In the Shadow of Idris, Ruth Kirtley  £4.99, 978 184427 374 4
Pilgrim, Eleanor Watkins  £4.99, 978 184427 373 7

## Fiction by Patricia St John

Rainbow Garden  £4.99, 978 184427 300 3
Star of Light  £4.99, 978 184427 296 9
The Mystery of Pheasant Cottage  £4.99, 978 184427 297 6
The Tanglewoods' Secret  £4.99, 978 184427 301 0
Treasures of the Snow  £5.99, 978 184427 298 3
Where the River Begins  £4.99, 978 184427 299 0

## Bible and Prayer

The 10 Must Know Stories, Heather Butler  £3.99, 978 184427 326 3
10 Rulz, Andy Bianchi  £4.99, 978 184427 053 8
Parabulz, Andy Bianchi  £4.99, 978 184427 227 3
Massive Prayer Adventure, Sarah Mayers  £4.99, 978 184427 211 2

## God and you!

No Girls Allowed, Darren Hill and Alex Taylor  £4.99, 978 184427 209 9
Friends Forever, Mary Taylor  £4.99, 978 184427 210 5

## Puzzle books

Bible Codecrackers: Moses, Valerie Hornsby  £3.99, 978 184427 181 8
Bible Codecrackers: Jesus, Gillian Ellis  £3.99, 978 184427 207 5
Bible Codecrackers: Peter & Paul, Gillian Ellis  £3.99, 978 184427 208 2

Available from your local Christian bookshop or from
Scripture Union Mail Order, PO Box 5148, Milton Keynes MLO, MK2 2YX
Tel: 0845 07 06 006 Website: www.scriptureunion.org.uk/shop
All prices correct at time of going to print.